Two-Timer

She stood there, rooted to the spot in total shock, her face draining of colour then suddenly glowing with a hectic flush as if the heating in the room had been turned up to double its current setting. He was gazing at her, too. They were connected by the power of that gaze as surely as if someone had passed a long rope around the wrist of each of them and linked them together. Viv felt a succession of tiny shivers ripple over the whole surface of her skin. Still she stared at him, still he stared back at her, equally unmoving … equally spellbound.

Who is he? she thought, her lips unconsciously framing the words as they formed in her mind. Who *is* he?

Point Romance

Two-Timer

Lorna Read

SCHOLASTIC

Scholastic Children's Books
7–9 Pratt Street, London NW1 0AE, UK
a division of Scholastic Publications Ltd,
London ~ New York ~ Toronto ~ Sydney ~ Auckland

First published by Scholastic Publications Ltd, 1995

Copyright © Lorna Read, 1995

ISBN 0 590 55930 3

Typeset by TW Typesetting, Midsomer Norton, Avon
Printed by Cox & Wyman Ltd, Reading, Berks.

1

"**O**h, wow! You look fantastic!"
The vision that greeted Viv as she opened her door could have stepped straight off the society pages of a posh magazine. Her heart beat faster as she took in his perfectly pressed dinner jacket and black trousers with the knife-edge crease. The ruffles which cascaded down the front of the dazzling white, spotless shirt which had been a fortunate find in a charity shop, lent a slightly rakish, artistic look to his ensemble, especially when coupled with his dark, wavy hair that always flopped over his forehead, even tonight when he had gelled it.

As her eyes swept him up and down, she noticed that his shoes were so highly polished she could have seen to comb her hair in their reflection. The sleek lines and trim cut of the outfit emphasized his height, which was six foot two, and his lean, wiry build.

"You don't look so bad yourself!" Jon responded, his warm brown eyes smiling into her hazel ones.

"Is that all you can say about me?" she said, with a mock hurt pout. She placed her hands on her hips and gave a twirl on the doorstep, which set the sequins shimmering on her figure-hugging scarlet dress. She had spent ages finding lipstick and nail polish in exactly the same shade of stunning red and her dark curls, normally held back in a ponytail, were tonight swept up on her head and decorated with a scarlet silk rose which had once adorned a hat of her mother's.

"Actually, I was lost for words. You look devastating. Incredible. Come here..." He swooped on her and was just about to plant his lips on hers when she shrieked and pushed him away.

"Careful! It took me ages to get my make-up right."

"Then allow me..." He took her hand, bowed gravely like a foreign prince greeting female royalty, and lifted her hand gently to his lips. He kissed the back of it, then turned it over and dropped another soft kiss in the palm. It sent goose-bumpy tingles right up her arms.

"I'll get my coat and you can escort me to my carriage." Viv indicated the taxi, the driver of which was busy scanning the sports pages of a newspaper in the dim glow shed by a street lamp.

It was seven-thirty on the night of Saturday, 18th January and for once, it was neither raining nor particularly cold. Viv and Jon were on their way to Viv's friend Fiona's eighteenth birthday party which was being held in the banqueting hall of the Otley Manor Hotel in Otley, a pretty village about five miles from the small Midlands town of Marshdale, where they lived. It was the first formal affair Viv had ever attended, though Jonathan had been to a couple of dinners connected with his father's business. He had hired his outfit, but Viv's mother had paid half towards hers, as part of her Christmas present.

In the taxi, Jon put his arm round Viv and she snuggled close to him. They had been going out together for almost two years now and Viv couldn't imagine a future which didn't contain him. The fact that, A-level grades permitting, he would be going off to university in the autumn was something that they were simply ignoring at present. Viv was slightly envious of him, though. She wished she would be leaving school in six months' time. But she, at seventeen, was a year younger than Jon and had another year at school to get through.

Three years apart! It didn't bear thinking about. Viv loved Jon and she knew he loved her. They had known each other since they were small children. They were part of each other's lives. Whatever happened, they could work it out.

"I know I said you looked fantastic, and I meant it, but there is one small thing wrong with the way you look," she told Jon.

"What do you mean?" he asked, sounding hurt.

"Your bow tie is blue."

"Huh?"

"Well, it would look much better if you wore one that matched my dress," she pointed out.

"How can I when I haven't got one?"

"You have now!" Viv said triumphantly and handed him a small package.

Jon tore the paper open with his teeth. Inside was a box with a cellophane lid. Through it glowed a scarlet bow tie on a black velvet ribbon with a velcro strip to fasten it. It had cost Viv more than she could afford, but it was a special occasion, after all – and she hoped this was just the first of many occasions on which they could dress up to the nines and feel like movie stars at an important première.

Jon gave Viv a lingering kiss on the cheek. "Thanks, Fluffy-head." That was his pet name for her. He removed his blue tie with a struggle and substituted the red one, and Viv helped him to tweak it straight.

"I shall feel really proud walking in with you tonight," she told him. "Everyone will wonder who my extremely handsome escort is –"

"– and you'll tell them it's only boring old Jon in disguise," he finished for her.

"Idiot!" She kissed him and left a scarlet imprint of her lips on his face. "Oops!" she said, scrabbling for a tissue in her bag and wiping it off.

"You should have left it there, it might have attracted a few more," Jon said mischievously.

"If you have any ideas about flirting, you can leave them behind in this taxi!" Viv snorted. She didn't really mean it. Loyalty could have been Jon's middle name.

Indeed, he proved it by going, "La, la-la-la, and I only have eyes for you…"

His voice cracked on the "you", sending Viv into

fits of giggles. Then the taxi pulled up and she hadn't even had time to feel nervous.

Scuffing her shoes through the thick carpet of the hotel corridor was a strange sensation for Viv, like walking through velvet sand. At the end of the corridor was a wooden easel bearing a large white sign which announced FIONA PAIGE IS 18 TODAY! in big red letters. A bunch of blue and pink balloons was tied to the corner. Fiona's dad was standing by the notice, greeting everybody.

"Quick, hold Fiona's present for me," said Viv, thrusting the large, heavy carrier bag containing a framed print for her friend's bedroom wall into Jon's hand. "I must go and straighten my hair and put some lipstick on."

"I'll meet you back here in half an hour then," Jon replied.

Viv gave him a "how-dare-you" grimace. "Five minutes!" she promised.

The Ladies was a-buzz with an excited babble of conversation. The fumes of hairspray and half a dozen different perfumes being applied simultaneously by aerosol made Viv gasp and flap the door to let some air in. She waved and called out "Hi!" to some girls she recognized.

Rosie Kingham was trying to fix the torn strap on her dress with a safety pin.

"I'll do it," offered Viv, marvelling at how everything Rosie wore always fell apart or, even worse, fell off.

"Would you? Oh, thanks. What does the back of my hair look like? Did you come with Jon?"

"Fine. And yes, who else?"

Nita Kemp, who had been earwigging on someone else's conversation as usual, piped up with, "I'll have him if you're getting fed up with him. It's time you had a change."

"Who asked you?" said Rosie, arching an already coal black eyebrow and making it even sootier. "Where's Trish?" she asked Viv.

"She's had to go to her aunt's silver wedding do. That was tonight as well. Isn't it a drag?" Trish was Viv's closest friend. Viv had promised to give her a detailed account of everything that happened at the party, omitting nothing.

"Your underskirt's showing," Rosie said, glancing at the hemline on Nita's short black velvet skirt.

"Rats!" shrieked Nita, then "Double rats!" when she discovered Rosie had been only kidding.

"You look really nice, Viv," Rosie said. It was true. The scarlet dress made Viv's skin look lush and creamy. With her shiny black curls and big, sparkling eyes, she looked glamorous and exotic, like a Spanish dancer. "What's that perfume?" she enquired.

Viv glanced at the spray in her hand. "You won't believe this but it's called Party Feelings," she laughed.

There was a loud snort from Nita. "There'll be a lot of those if the lights go out," she sniggered.

"You've got a one-track mind, Kempy," said Rosie.

"Yes, the dirt-track. That's an old one," Nita fired back.

"Are you two ready? Come on then. Let's all arrive together for moral support," suggested Viv.

"*Im*moral support," supplied the irrepressible Nita.

Jon was waiting patiently by the signboard when the girls arrived. He was talking to Colin Gray, who was Rosie's date for the night, but the two guys broke off their conversation and stood to attention as the girls appeared. Colin gave a low wolf-whistle which earned him a dig in the ribs from Rosie's elbow.

Jon put an arm round Viv's waist and swept her into the Banqueting Hall with a flourish. As they walked in, they had to give their names to an usher, who announced them as if they were royalty.

"Jonathan Hammond and Vivienne McCulloch."

There was an immediate chorus of hellos from the friends who were thronging around Fiona as she opened her presents. Fiona was looking stunning in a strapless dress of deep green taffeta which set off her heavy, shining chestnut hair, and long drop earrings which flashed green and silver sparkles.

Jon went to hand Viv the bag containing Fiona's present.

"No, you give it to her. It's from both of us," Viv whispered.

"But I haven't—"

"Ssh. Just give it to her."

Jon had promised to give Viv some money towards Fiona's gift, but he was so busy swotting for his A-levels that he had had to give up his Saturday job in a high street shoe store and consequently was extremely broke. He couldn't even afford to run his car at present.

7

"Now let me guess ... it's a cassette. No, it's a teddy bear," joked Fiona, feeling the parcel.

"Wrong. It's a packet of..." Viv had been about to say "chewing gum" but at that moment something happened which drove the words right out of her brain. Her eyes had flicked across the room and come to rest on a boy, and even a ribald suggestion from Fiona's boyfriend Steve as to what it might be a packet of failed to register, though everyone else hooted with laughter.

She stood there, rooted to the spot in total shock, her face draining of colour then suddenly glowing with a hectic flush as if the heating in the room had been turned up to double its current setting. He was gazing at her, too. They were connected by the power of that gaze as surely as if someone had passed a long rope around the wrist of each of them and linked them together. Viv felt a succession of tiny shivers ripple over the whole surface of her skin. Still she stared at him, still he stared back at her, equally unmoving ... equally spellbound.

Who is he? she thought, her lips unconsciously framing the words as they formed in her mind. Who *is* he?

2

How do you describe the moment when you see a total stranger and *know*, just know, that you and he are meant to be together? All the sounds going on around Viv, of music, excited conversation, children yelling, Fiona thanking her for the lovely present, became muted as her surroundings swirled away, leaving nobody in the room but herself and that boy.

A moist film of tears blurred his image and when Viv looked again he had gone. But her memory of him was as strong as if he were still standing there with his thick, corn-coloured hair tied back in a ponytail, a hint of sexy stubble on his chin and eyes the colour of a cloudless sky at midnight.

How do I know his eyes are dark blue when I'm not close enough to see, Viv wondered. Yet, as certainly as if she had met him before, she knew.

"Are you all right, Viv?" asked Fiona, staring at her with concern in her eyes.

Viv blinked, clearing the mist. She was suddenly

aware that her mouth was open and gaping like a fish in a trance, so she closed it with a decisive snap that hurt her teeth, and nodded energetically.

"Yes thanks, I'm fine."

"She went all peculiar for a minute, Jon," Fiona said.

"She needs some food and drink inside her," said Jon. "Don't you, Viv?"

Viv agreed that she did. But she also knew that she wanted to go over to the heavily laden buffet table on her own, with no boyfriend accompanying her. She had to find that boy again; had to make an impression on him as a girl on her own, a girl he stood a chance with.

But you're not alone, you're not free. You've got a steady boyfriend, nagged the voice of her conscience. *He's probably got a girlfriend, anyway.*

He couldn't have ... he mustn't have! He had been put on this earth for her alone.

You're mad – totally mad! Viv told herself firmly. *Stop behaving like a stupid adolescent.*

She couldn't join in the conversations happening all around her. Everything seemed disjointed and disconnected, as if she had already drunk two or three glasses of champagne. Her eyes scanned the room feverishly. Where was he? *Who* was he?

Agitated and confused, she untucked her arm from Jon's. "Tell you what, I'll go over and load up a plate and we can both pick off it, while you get us some drinks," she suggested. It was a ploy to get away alone and have another look at The Vision.

"OK," he agreed. "Get us a seat and I'll come and find you."

Viv darted off like an arrow released from a bow. She felt light, as if she were floating across the room towards the snowy white tablecloth and the heaped bowls and platters. A few minutes, that was all she had. She grabbed a plate and loaded it up, scarcely noticing what she put on it, mixing ham and salmon, sausage rolls and rice-with-things-in and topping the lot with chopped lettuce. She added a dollop of Thousand Island for good measure, then bore her trophy away, planning to skirt the room, ostensibly in search of a place to sit down and eat but really searching for him.

"You're never going to get through all that by yourself, surely? You'll lose that lovely figure!"

The voice was caressing, husky, amused, and came from somewhere behind her left shoulder. Viv didn't dare turn her head in case it wasn't ... in case it was.

It was. "I'm ... I'm getting some for some other people, too. A kind of communal plateful," she explained feebly.

She had to force herself to speak when all she wanted to do was gaze – at that strong face, the square jaw, the nose with the cute bump on it, the eyebrows that held glints of gold, and those eyes which were just the colour she had imagined, like midnight blue velvet.

"Where do you know Fiona from?" he enquired.

"School." She hated having to admit it as it made her feel horribly young. It was as if a gulf existed between them which separated the adult world, to which he obviously belonged, from the world of textbooks and lessons. How was she to bridge it?

"I left school when I was sixteen. I was a bit of a rebel, I'm afraid," he said. When he smiled, a tiny dimple appeared in his chin. Viv watched it, fascinated.

"So what do you do now?" she asked.

"I'm in the music business."

"I'm impressed," Viv said admiringly. Her heart was racing, beating so strongly that she wondered if the front of her dress was visibly pulsating. The loaded plate in her hand felt terribly heavy. Fearful of dropping it, she put it back down on the table.

"Can I get you a drink?" he asked.

"Er..." If only he could, she thought. If only Jon would get talking to someone and stay away for the next half hour. She could see him talking to one of the bar staff, ordering their drinks. It wouldn't be long before he would be looking for her. He would come walking up with two glasses of white wine and make it horribly obvious that he was her boyfriend.

"I'd love one, but I'm afraid my friends are waiting for this," she said, picking up the plate again.

"See you later, then?" he asked, sounding purposeful, as if he really meant it.

"Hope so." Don't sound too keen, she told herself. Don't behave like a star-struck idiot.

Reluctantly, she went back to the group around

Fiona. She got back before Jon. That gave her the chance she wanted.

"Who's that blond guy with the ponytail?" she asked Fiona.

"The one in the linen suit? That's Shane Russell, he's a mate of the guy who's doing the disco. They're sharing the job between them. Nice, isn't he?"

"Mm," Viv grunted. She had to sound non-committal because Jon had just returned.

"You're not eating," he pointed out.

She picked up a chicken leg and pretended to nibble it, but her stomach was turning somersaults. Shane ... Shane Russell. I suppose being a DJ was what he meant by being in the music business, she told herself and smiled, thinking of how she had glamourized him into being a record producer, if not the lead singer with a band.

Still, deejaying is part of the music business really, so he didn't lie, she realized. Anyway, what would I have said if he'd asked me what I did, and hadn't known I was still at school? she wondered. She decided she'd have said, "I'm a student," and hoped he'd think she was older, and already at college.

There was no chance of looking for Shane for a while as there were too many friends to talk to. Then Jon asked her to dance. She went automatically into his arms as she had done so many times before. She loved dancing with Jon. He had a perfect sense of rhythm and over the two years they had been together, they'd learned how to move in harmony. In slow dances, Jon propelled her with the lightest of pressure and she felt like a feather in his arms, nestling close to his firm chest, feeling the sexy heat of his arms burning across her back.

Halfway through this dance, which was the old number, *Don't It Make My Brown Eyes Blue*, Viv suddenly felt a prickling at the back of her neck and over her head, as if someone were staring at her very hard. It was difficult to turn round as her face was jammed against Jon's, but she managed to swivel her eyes – and they met a pair of deep blue ones gazing intensely at her.

Excited heat swept her body and a surge of energy filled her limbs. She pulled away from Jon and executed a slow spin, then moved in close to him again. She felt as if she were dancing in a competition with the television cameras on her. She knew she was showing off but she didn't care. She was dancing for an audience of one.

"What's with the fancy footwork?" Jon asked, gazing at her admiringly. "Been taking secret lessons?"

"No. I just felt inspired," she explained truthfully.

Once the record had finished, she made for the seclusion of the Ladies to splash cold water on her hot cheeks and calm down a little. Liz, Fiona's cousin, was in there, squinting myopically at the mirror from a distance of about ten centimetres and putting on a fresh coat of lipstick.

"Enjoying it?" Liz asked.

"Oh, yes!" answered Viv enthusiastically. Some tendrils of hair were coming down and she poked and prodded them back into place and fixed her drooping silk rose.

"He's really good-looking, your boyfriend. Wish I was ten years younger, I'd fight you for him!" joked Liz.

Viv smiled. She didn't really feel like talking. She wanted to think. About Jon ... about Shane. Every time she pictured those blue eyes, that thick, unruly fair hair, that brilliant, sexy smile, she felt shaky and excited and strange, as if she were standing on top of a high building, dangerously close to the edge, looking out over a distant, beautiful landscape.

What's happening to me? she asked herself. I shouldn't be feeling like this. I'm with Jon. I haven't felt a thing for another boy since I met him.

But you do now, that other, uncontrollable side of her brain announced.

This is stupid, she told herself. Pull yourself together, McCulloch! Grow up! He's just an ordinary guy – a rather good-looking one, to be sure, but nothing to lose your head about.

So why are you acting like a Mills & Boon heroine? mocked that other voice.

Viv shook her head and more dark tendrils tumbled from her crown. This time she couldn't be bothered to tidy them.

"Are you all right?" Liz was giving her a strange look and Viv realized she'd been rooted to the spot as if in a trance.

"Yes," she replied. "Just got a few things on my mind, that's all."

Liz put away her lipstick, walked towards the door, paused, said, "Good luck," and finally left Viv alone. She took a deep, deep breath, then let it out in a shuddering sigh. Get a grip, she ordered herself. Don't even look at Shane. I'm with Jon, the boy I love. He's waiting for me. He must be wondering what's happened to me by now.

She fixed a bright smile on to her face, left the Ladies, walked briskly down the carpeted corridor – and bumped right into Shane who was coming through the swing doors.

"Oh!" Viv gasped, her composure completely collapsing.

"Hello again!" he said, treating her to another of those slow, radiant, devastating smiles. "I'm really glad I bumped into you now because I've got to do the disco in a minute and I mightn't get another chance to talk to you. Do you like music?"

"Love it!" said Viv, with all the enthusiasm she could muster.

"What kind?"

"Most things, really. I'm bored with a lot of the rap and house that's around, though I like some. I like funky dance music, some heavy rock—"

"You like heavy metal?" he interrupted eagerly. "That's great. Because I was going to ask you if you'd come to a gig at the Five Stars next Thursday. It'll be a real thrash, I promise."

He was smiling at her and she raised her face to his smile like a flower to the sun. She felt like a puppet on invisible strings. He could pull her any way she wanted, she had no control. All she was

was an emotional reaction standing precariously on legs through which a fine tremor was running. Her arms had come up in goose-pimples, just through being near him.

"Who's playing?" she asked. Oh, why did she have to go through this pretence of deciding whether she wanted to go or not? It didn't matter what band was on. Why didn't she just say yes and have done with it?

As soon as she heard the reply, though, she was glad she'd asked.

"Me," he said.

3

When she awoke the morning after the party, Viv was amazed to realize that she had, in fact, slept. How could she have done, with so many confused and tormented thoughts rushing round inside her brain? She stretched and listened to the sound of the radio playing in the kitchen beneath her bedroom, where her mother would be eating her breakfast. Her father would be out. He went over to his brother Brian's most Sundays as he was helping him to restore an old car he'd bought.

Am I happy, or am I too worried to be happy? she asked herself. She honestly didn't know. For so long she had thought only about Jon. While her friends had been keeping their eye out for new, available boys to date, Viv's own "eye" had been well shut for two whole years. Until now.

I can't go out with Shane, I can't. *I mustn't!* she ordered herself fiercely. But she wanted to. A little worm was at work in her brain, like the kind you sometimes find inside apples, boring a brown hole in the sweet fruit and spoiling it; but instead of an apple, it was her relationship with Jon which was going to be affected. The worm was telling her that going out with Jon was getting ever so slightly boring, that she needed fresh excitement in her life. It was telling her that she wasn't really, truly in love with Jon for ever and ever.

I am, I am. I do love him! she wailed inside her head. *Of course I do.*

"Maybe it's got to be a habit," said the worm of doubt. "Perhaps you should try going out with another boy just once, to see what's it like, so you can see your relationship with Jon objectively, as it really is."

There was danger in that, Viv knew. Lots of danger. Once again, she experienced the feeling she'd had the previous evening, as if she were standing on top of a high building in a force ten gale. No, even better, sitting beside a racing driver who was hurtling round a bend at a hundred and fifty miles per hour! She felt reckless and brave and adventurous, ready for something new. She didn't want to hurt Jon, but this was something different, something totally outside her relationship with him, something which felt a little like a holiday. One date ... yes, it was a mini-holiday. No one need ever know.

Then, shocked, she checked her runaway thoughts. How *could* she be thinking like this? Oh, poor Jon! She was a horrible person, she didn't deserve him. He was the perfect boyfriend, handsome, kind, considerate, thoughtful... She couldn't possibly be unfaithful to him!

But just one secret date that he'd never know about... What was wrong with that...? *No, NO!* screamed her conscience.

In this tortured state she finally trailed downstairs to breakfast. Her mother took one look at her wan face and asked, "Have you got a hangover, dear?"

Viv leapt at this excuse for her silence. "Yes, a bit," she lied.

"Serves you right," stated her mother, deciding to leave her alone to recover.

Thus spared, Viv was able to spend the morning brooding.

Jon was coming round later. As the clock ticked closer to six, Viv's guilt grew stronger and stronger as thoughts of Shane refused to leave her mind.

Was just one date with another bloke being unfaithful? Viv wondered. Couldn't she tell Jon about Shane's invitation and assure him that there was nothing in it, that he'd just asked her to come along and listen to his band? Jon would never want to come. He hated heavy metal.

Oh, if only he wasn't coming round tonight, she thought. She had so much on her mind that she would rather have an evening to herself to think everything over.

In the end, she decided to ring Jon and put him off, but luckily she was spared the problem of having to think of an excuse because Jon's mother answered and said she was glad Viv had rung because it had saved her a phone call. Jon was in bed ill – he'd had a bad stomach all day.

Although she felt sorry for him, Viv felt as

though a heavy weight had been lifted off her head, leaving her light and floaty. She didn't have to think about Jon tonight. She was free to dream about Shane and the exciting date which must remain her secret…

Monday, Tuesday, Wednesday … how they dragged. Jon was still feeling ill. He'd croaked down the phone that he thought it was either gastric flu or the prawns, but she'd eaten prawns too and she was all right.

She sent him a funny "Get Well" card. It was strange, going so long without seeing him – he'd told her not to come round in case he had a bug and she caught it. In all the time they'd been going out, it was rare for them to spend more than two or three days apart, except when they went on holiday with their respective families.

She felt strangely disorientated without him. She missed him, of course she did, she told herself adamantly, but that feeling stayed steady, like a dull toothache that never reached the point of agony, but never went away, always simmering in the background. The feeling that overlaid it and grew stronger every day was that of guilt. There was poor Jon, coughing and sweating feverishly in hot, rumpled bedclothes, having his temperature taken by his mother at frequent intervals and having pills and lemon drinks forced down him. She could imagine the whole scene because Jon had told her how his mother fussed over him. She'd become ten times worse since her divorce from Jon's dad.

Somehow, knowing that he was safely ensconced in his sick bed enabled her to put their relationship on mental ice for a while and get on with thinking, guiltily yet excitedly, about Shane and fantasizing about what might happen on their date. Would she still like him or would she, as often happened on first dates, find he wasn't as nice as she'd expected? Would he want to kiss her? Would she want to see him again? It would cause a few problems in her life if she did!

Then at last it was Thursday and suddenly Jon was better. He rang her in the morning before she left for school and said, "Let's go to a movie tonight."

Without a second's hesitation, Viv found herself lying. "Sorry, I can't. I didn't know if you'd be better so I promised to go round to Trish's."

She felt her cheeks flaming and was glad they were talking on the phone rather than face to face. Could he tell from her voice that she wasn't telling the truth? She hoped not. She hated lying to him but, on the other hand, it wasn't as if she was going to get up to anything with Shane. It was just curiosity that was urging her to meet him, nothing else. It wasn't as if she was going to let him *kiss* her...

One problem which occurs with monotonous regularity in every girl's life is the one known as "what am I going to wear?" As soon as she got home from school, Viv dragged out the contents of drawers and wardrobes and tried on jeans with various combinations of tops, all of which looked completely wrong. Then she tried a dress but it looked too fussy for a pub. Skirts, shorts, leggings, shirts and T-shirts were tossed into a jumbled heap on the bed. Some fell off on to the floor and tangled round Viv's ankle, sending her flying into her wicker bedroom chair with a shriek of pain.

A blue, throbbing bruise on her arm did nothing to improve her frantic mood. Shane had said the band were on at half past eight, then again at ten. She wanted to get there early, so she could stand near the front and see them play. But if she didn't find something to wear soon, she'd never get there at all!

In a state approaching panic, Viv hauled on her jeans again, shrugged her way into a Save the Dolphin sweatshirt, shoved her feet into her Nike trainers, grabbed her black leather jacket and a red woolly scarf, looked at herself in the mirror and despaired. Was that pale-faced, straggly-haired, boringly-dressed girl really her? How could Shane possibly fancy her looking like this? He'd only seen her in the sexy red dress. He was going to be really disappointed.

Her heart felt so heavy that she could scarcely breathe. She kicked at a pile of clothes, hating them. Hating herself, her hair, her shortness – when she'd always wanted to be tall and leggy and model-like.

Full of gloom, she caught the bus. When she got off it at the pub and saw the poster advertising *Bombshell*, Shane's band, she felt so sick with nerves that she almost caught the next bus back home again. Did I feel like this on my first date with Jon? she wondered. She honestly couldn't remember, it was so long ago.

She paused in the doorway of the pub, hearing the buzz of talk and laughter and the thump of the jukebox coming in waves through the door as people went in and out. I can't go in, she thought, terrified. It was the first time in her life that she had ever had to go into a pub where she didn't know anybody. She couldn't do it. People would stare at her. Men would think she wanted to be picked up.

But I *do* know somebody, she reminded herself. I know Shane. Well, almost...

She thought of the very last time she'd seen him the previous Saturday, as he was helping his partner to dismantle the equipment and pack it away. Jon had had his arm round her and she had turned and caught Shane's eye. He had looked at her – a long, steady look as if he were probing her mind to try and find out what was going on between her and Jon.

He hadn't smiled, hadn't winked, nothing like that. Just that long, cool, searching gaze which had made her feel hot and tingly inside. The way he looked was etched on her memory. The macho stubble, the blue eyes, the thick blond hair in its ponytail.

Taking a deep breath and squaring her shoulders bravely, she pushed open the heavy swing doors of the pub and walked in.

4

She saw him immediately, leaning on the bar, his right hand curled around a pint glass. He caught sight of her and beckoned and her heart gave a dizzying lurch.

"Hi, Viv! I'm really glad you could come," he called. He smiled and it was as if someone had turned the light on in a dark room. Beams of light seemed to dance out of his eyes. Viv thought she had never seen a smile like it, which took over its owner so completely. Her legs were turning to jelly.

"What are you drinking?" he asked.

"Er ... just a mineral water please, with ice and lemon."

He didn't scoff and try and force an alcoholic drink on her as some boys would have done. He simply accepted her request without comment and ordered her mineral water. When it came, he handed it to her, saying, "I'll have to go in a sec. I hung on as long as I could, hoping to see you before we went on, but we're due to start any minute. Will you be all right on your own?"

"Yes, fine," she heard herself say, as if from a great distance. This whole scene felt unreal. Her, in a strange pub, with a male who wasn't Jon, about to listen to a band she'd never heard and knew nothing about. She pinched the skin on the back of her hand between her right thumb and index finger. It hurt. So she wasn't dreaming!

"There's a seat at that table over there, near the stage," Shane told her. He stood up and helped her down from the high bar stool, then walked over to the table with her and pulled out the chair for her to sit down.

Viv had always thought Jon had good manners, but Shane was even more polite, Viv reflected as, with a "See you later," he strode off to join the group who were plugging in various pieces of equipment.

A man walked up to the microphone in front of the instruments and announced, "Ladies and gentlemen, let's have a big hand for tonight's band, *Bombshell*!" He skipped down from the low stage while a smattering of expectant applause broke out.

There was a loud roll on the drums, a whine of feedback from an electric guitar, and the pub exploded with sound. Heavy wasn't the word. The rhythm they pounded out was the type to set foundations quaking and high buildings tumbling.

Viv's hands flew to her ears but she forced them back on to her lap again. She didn't want Shane thinking she was a wimp. But the sound really hurt. She was sitting too close to the speakers. Then she had an inspiration. She fumbled in her bag, found a paper tissue, tore off two scraps, kneaded them into balls and sneaked them under her long hair and into her ears.

Yes, this was much better! Now it wasn't all one great crashing cacophony, for she could tell the sounds apart, hear Shane's bass, and the keyboard, and the singer, who also played lead guitar, struggling to make himself heard above everybody else.

Shane looked gorgeous. His denim shirt was open to the waist and his chest was smooth, lightly tanned and gleaming. She felt her fingertips tingling with the longing to reach out and touch him. A fine gold chain with a tiny cross on it glinted against his skin. She scarcely noticed the other guys in the band, she was so captivated with him.

He looked at her and gave a little jerk of his head and a smile. It made Viv feel special. Out of all the girls here tonight, she was the one he was smiling at. Suddenly, she stopped listening critically to the sound and began to enjoy herself. Shane sang harmonies with the lead singer, but there was one song which he sang alone. It was a quiet, slow, wistful number a bit out of keeping with the band's normal heaviness, and Shane's voice was husky and tuneful. It did something to her, made the tiny hairs stand up right down her arms.

The song obviously wasn't to the taste of most of

the audience, who were dedicated heavy metal freaks, but Viv loved it and clapped loudly even though hardly anyone else bothered to.

"Well, what did you think?" asked Shane after their set was over, and they were back leaning on the bar together. He was glistening with sweat, the back of his hair was damp and frizzy with it. Viv could smell the faint, exciting aroma of his hot body. Her eyes strayed to the array of gleaming bottles at the back of the bar and the framed photograph of the bar staff being presented with a trophy.

She brought her eyes back to Shane. What did he expect her to say? That they were utterly, completely brilliant? They weren't – but he was!

"It was a bit too loud for me," she confessed. "I suppose that's because it's a small place and you've got big amplifiers."

She was pleased that she'd managed to sound knowledgeable and technical and was rewarded with a thoughtful nod from Shane.

"Go on," he pressed. "What else?"

"The songs... I didn't know a lot of them but they were really good. Especially the slow ones."

"I wrote most of them," he confessed. He raised his glass to his lips and took a deep draught of cold golden lager. Viv watched the way his throat moved when he swallowed. She longed to plant a little feathery kiss just there, on his Adam's apple.

"Even the slow ones?" she enquired. She had to know. The slow numbers had all been love songs.

"Particularly the slow ones. But I haven't

written a new one for ages. I have to be in love..."

Viv's eyebrows shot up and her heart began to hammer. This meant there couldn't be anybody else in his life at present ... that the way was clear for her. Her other life, with Jon, was utterly forgotten as she gave herself up totally to finding out more about Shane and getting closer to him. It was a whole new world to explore. Meeting a new person was like opening the pages of a novel. A detective novel in some cases, where you couldn't take what the person said at face value but had to read between the lines and search for clues.

Though Shane seemed open and straight-forward enough.

Viv asked him what he did when he wasn't either singing or helping out his DJ friend.

"I'm a student," was the surprise answer.

"No! I don't believe it! I thought you couldn't wait to leave school! Where are you studying?"

"At the computer college in Salisbury Street. After I left school, it dawned on me that I mightn't become a superstar after all and I'd be better off having a few qualifications. What are you studying?"

"Languages. German, French and Russian. I hope to go to university next year."

"I hope you make it," Shane said, taking another long pull on his pint. He put the glass back on the bar without looking, placed it half on the edge of the ashtray and it tipped, sending a stream of foaming lager shooting over the edge of the bar towards him. He jumped, then laughed.

"Look at that. You're making me nervous!" he joked.

"*Me?*" chuckled Viv, feeling the tense lump in her throat dissolve. She had never considered the fact that he might be as tensed up as she was on their first date – if you could call this a date.

"You must be pretty brainy to be studying computers. I can just about use one but I'd never be able to write programs for them or anything," she confessed.

He started talking about computer logic and what computers of the future would be able to do. As he talked, Viv studied him. How different from Jon he was. Even his movements were different. Jon was taller and more finely built, yet his movements and gestures, far from being graceful, were uncoordinated and jerky. Shane was powerful and broadshouldered and square-handed, yet there was a rhythm and a grace in the way he moved that made him seem at ease in the space around him, and in complete control of his body.

She shut her eyes for an instant, overwhelmed by the physical attraction she felt for him. She imagined those powerful arms closing round her, pulling her towards that broad, strong chest. She could feel the graze of his stubble against the skin of her face, she could taste the salt of his skin on her lips...

"We've got to go on again now. See you later."

He was gone, swigging the last gulp of beer, striding towards the front of the room.

The second set was even louder than the first. The sound mix was so bad that everything sounded distorted and Viv had to plug her ears again. Even if she couldn't listen properly, she could at least see, and watching Shane made the ordeal worthwhile.

At last the band were packing up and people were leaving. Viv felt vulnerable and conspicuous, hugging her drink while all around her people were saying their goodnights and walking out of the doors. Where was he? She decided to give him another five minutes and if he didn't appear, she would go home. But all at once he was there, walking across the emptying room towards her. Her heart gave a lurch at the sight of him and she nearly dropped her glass. He was smiling that devastating smile.

"Do you need a lift home?" he asked her.

"Yes, please," she replied.

He had a rusty old white van. As far as Viv was concerned, he could have driven a milk float so long as she was alone in it with him. When they reached her road, she asked him to stop a few houses away, in case her parents happened to glance out of the window.

They sat and talked for a while. "I thought you might be going out with that bloke you were at the party with," Shane said suddenly.

Viv stiffened, feeling a guilty blush threatening that was bound to give her away. She dug her nails into the palms of her hands, desperately trying to keep cool. Her stomach gave an uncomfortable lurch, as if she was standing on the deck of a ship in high seas.

Oh, Jon, she thought, please don't be listening

in to my thoughts. I don't want to hurt you. A picture of his kind, handsome, smiling face dropped in front of her eyes as if somebody had placed a photograph there. She felt paralysed by guilt and indecision. What could she tell Shane that wouldn't put him off, yet wouldn't make her feel she was denying her relationship with Jon, which was still so very much alive?

Shane was staring at her, waiting. The silence between them was so tense, it was almost solid, like a thick pane of glass.

"You kissed him," he prompted.

"Y-yes, I did," she faltered. "But it's not what it seemed. We've known each other for years. We're ... very good friends, that's all."

"That's good," Shane murmured. "I just wanted to find out where I stood. So – the coast is clear!"

He smiled a smile so wide and dazzling and wholehearted that Viv felt buffeted by the waves of warmth that came her way. She was trying to recover when he slid his arm thrillingly round her shoulders, pulled her to him and kissed her.

Viv had been kissed many times by Jon, whom she'd always thought was a wonderful kisser, with the power to make her go hot and shivery right down to her shoes. Jon's kisses were passionate, yet familiar. She knew them so well that she knew what to expect when his lips reached out to hers and she surrendered her mouth to his happily, confident that he'd kiss her just enough, but not too much.

But now she was back on that pitching, tossing boat, with her stomach lurching. Shane's kiss was full of subtle variations and she sensed danger, and was afraid. It was a sneaky kiss, starting off gentle, the merest brush of lip on lip, and then becoming gradually firmer, catching her up in its skilful pressure, sending her pulses rocketing and making her pant and go all useless and floppy. And even more anxious and afraid.

Their kiss was like a dance, with his lips pressing forward, while hers retreated, then she leading while he followed. He seemed to anticipate every move and be ready with a move of his own. It was totally intoxicating and she could have gone on kissing him for ever – yet at the same time she was anxious for him to stop. She couldn't take it. It shouldn't be happening at all. She had no right to enjoy it. She felt completely out of her depth.

In panic, she opened her eyes wide and looked over his shoulder. The clock on his dashboard said 12.25. Oh, no! She had no idea it was so late. She had to go home or she'd be in trouble.

"What's wrong?" Shane asked, feeling her tense up in his arms.

"I've got to go," she gasped.

"OK," he said, and flashed her that warm smile again.

She felt prissy and awkward as she pulled the strap of her bag over her shoulder and rearranged her hair. She was sure he was seeing her as the schoolgirl she still was, and not taking her very seriously. This was just a casual thing for him, she thought; another notch on his scorecard. Something to boast about to his friends – "I've got this little schoolgirl who's mad about me and the band. She's a groupie."

No, he wouldn't want to see her again. This one kissing session would be enough. He wasn't the kind of guy who'd want to go out with someone who was always diving off home early because of lessons the next day. He didn't understand, he wasn't like Jon. Jon and she had much more in common.

"Can I see you again?"

Her heart leapt into her mouth. Jon's face flashed in front of her eyes, his familiar serious expression, his lovely dark, floppy, shiny hair. He meant so much to her, he'd been in her life for so long. He was her dearest friend as well as being her boyfriend. He understood her so well, fitted in with her life, knew what she was all about, respected her need to study and complete homework projects. As she thought about Jon and how gorgeous and kind and lovable he was, she was flooded with warm feelings towards him. This situation with Shane was crazy. She already had the best boyfriend any girl could have. It wasn't fair to lead Shane on as it couldn't go anywhere. She was never going to finish with Jon. She had to let Shane down gently. Right now.

Then she looked at his open, hopeful face … looked again into those dancing, dazzling, questioning eyes. How could she say no, even if it meant lying to Jon again? So she whispered, "Yes."

5

As she waited for Jon to come round the next night, Viv hoped that nothing showed on her face. She felt as if Shane's kiss was still printed there for all the world to see. Would Jon see any change in her? Was there some minute thing about her that might give the game away? She felt more and more nervous and agitated as the minutes ticked away. Every time she heard footsteps in the street, she clenched her fists and tensed her shoulders, until she was starting to develop a headache.

Then Jon arrived and it was if she had been dropped on to a familiar stage set and knew all the lines. Last night vanished as she slotted back into the familiar role of Jon's girlfriend. It was easy, she found. She asked him how he was now, they chatted about school and went for a pizza to the place they normally went to. And Viv had her usual Four Seasons while Jon had his habitual American Hot.

Then, right in the middle of taking a mouthful, something weird happened. It was a kind of flashback to the previous evening, which she had thought she'd successfully banished to some strongroom in the back of her mind. She glanced at Jon and for an instant, seemed to see Shane's face superimposed over his, blue eyes over brown, fair hair over dark, craggier features and a hint of stubble over Jon's lean, cleancut looks. She stared, mesmerized, until the vision swam and became ordinary, familiar Jon again. But it had given her a terrible jolt and her heart was racing.

"Penny for them," Jon said, seeing that Viv had gone into an apparent trance with her fork halfway to her lips. "Is something wrong with your pizza?"

"No. The pizza's great. It's ... it's homework, that's all. I keep thinking about this essay," she invented hastily, hating herself for lying.

"I finished mine. I got a B-plus."

"Well done! I'm sure you're going to get a Grade A for all your A-levels. I'll probably scrape by with Ds and Es." Keep to safe topics, she told herself. That way she wouldn't feel so bad, or give anything away.

"I'll still love you even if you fail everything," Jon reassured her, which made her feel worse again.

Then he began chatting about family things – his older sister in Australia who was having another baby, his mother accidentally locking the cat in the boxroom – and things slowly returned to something more like normality and Viv felt herself slotting back into their relationship like a plant resettling its roots after having been dug up. She could almost forget Shane, if it wasn't for the fact that the young waiter serving them at the Pasta Palace had fair hair and blue eyes almost exactly the same shade as his.

When Jon took her home afterwards, Viv invited him into the living-room for a coffee. Her mother insisted on making it and bustled out to the kitchen. As soon as she'd vanished and the door had clicked shut behind her, Jon took Viv into his arms.

"Oh, Viv, I've really missed you. Do you realize we haven't seen each other for a week?" he said. "I've missed this, too..." he added, reaching for her lips.

A wave of vertigo assailed Viv. The room seemed to lurch as she was pitchforked back into her memories of the previous night, in the car with Shane. She had a strong sense of déjà vu in the split second before Jon's lips met hers, remembering how she had been poised in a similar moment the previous evening, before Shane had kissed her for the first time. Jon's lips ... Shane's lips... How could two sets of lips feel so different against hers?

And how could she find Shane's kiss so exciting, yet now be totally swept up in these warm, melting feelings for Jon? For his kiss was doing wonderful things to her. Safe in these strong, familiar arms, she reacted the way she had always reacted – with fervour and passion, giving back everything he was giving her, and more. How could she do it? Wasn't she just the most wicked, cruel, heartless girl who ever existed?

She felt herself stagger slightly, and caught at Jon's jacket.

"What's wrong?" he asked, breaking off the kiss.

"I ... sort of lost my balance," she said weakly.

"It was my wonderful, passionate kiss making you dizzy with desire," said Jon, half teasing and half serious.

"You're right," she answered teasingly, thinking, oh, Jon was so sweet, so gorgeous. She did love him, she really did. She put her arms round him and gave him a hug.

But after he had gone and she was lying in bed on the point of slipping into sleep, she found herself comparing those kisses again. Who had the softest lips, Jon or Shane? Who kissed the best? And did technique matter, anyway? Surely what mattered was her feelings while she was being kissed, not the kiss itself? She had lived and re-lived Shane's kiss until her lips had encountered Jon's again and now she felt thoroughly confused because she was lying here loving Jon, wanting him, not being able to get enough of kissing him and being in his arms.

If only there was someone she could talk to. She felt awful keeping it back from Trish, but she knew her friend would disapprove. Trish thought Jon was an amazing catch and was quite jealous of the fact that their relationship had lasted so long while her own always seemed to break up after a few weeks. She would think Viv was totally mad if she confessed to fancying another boy; she might be so livid that she'd be tempted to tell Jon.

Rosie? Fiona? Nita? No, nobody could be trusted to keep a secret as red hot as this one. She didn't want to hear herself gossiped about all over school. She could just imagine what people would say: "You know Viv McCulloch? She's been going out with Jon for two years and now she's two-timing him with some boy who plays in a band!"

No, this double life of hers was one she couldn't share with anyone. Not without taking the risk that some teeny shred of her deceit might filter back to Jon...

The following night she and Shane met for a drink in a pub in the town centre. Viv was worried that she might bump into someone she knew, but the place was nearly empty and they were able to have a quiet but interesting time sampling some of the many varieties of cider the bar specialized in.

He walked her back to the bus stop afterwards. He hadn't brought the van as he knew he would be drinking that evening.

"Sorry I can't take you home," he apologized. His own bus home went in a totally different direction from hers.

"That's OK," said Viv. Inwardly, she was thinking *thank goodness*. Just imagine if she had been expected to ask him in for coffee when she got home? That could have been very awkward indeed.

"I'll be rehearsing most of the weekend and we've got a gig on Monday night, but come round to my place on Sunday afternoon," Shane had said. He scribbled his address on a scrap of paper torn off an envelope he'd had in his pocket. *59C Shawbury Place, Marsden End*, he had written.

"Ring the middle bell and if there's no reply, knock very loudly because sometimes the bell doesn't work," he explained.

Then he put his arms round her and gently but firmly kissed her. One bus came and went, followed by another one, while they were still kissing.

When the third bus rolled up, Viv said reluctantly that she had better go.

"See you Sunday!" Shane said. She found a seat and looked out of the window and felt a stab of disappointment when she saw him walking off in the direction of his own bus stop. Why hadn't he stayed and waved goodbye like Jon always did?

But Shane *isn't* Jon, she reminded herself. He could hardly be expected to behave in the same way. Jon and she were an established couple. He knew what little gestures made her happy.

And he loves me, she reminded herself. Thinking about Jon, picturing his serious, sincere face looking wistful as he waved goodbye, made her smile to herself. He'd promised to go for a walk in the country with her tomorrow. That was something they often did on a Saturday afternoon, taking rucksacks containing sandwiches and drinks and heading for home as soon as it started to get dark. And on Sunday evening he'd promised to take her to a new film that was on at the Cannon cinema.

Sunday? Oh no! Viv's hand shot to her mouth in alarm. She was seeing Shane on Sunday. How could she have forgotten about her date with Jon when she'd agreed to go round to Shane's? It was as if her brain was split into two separate compartments, one of which was devoted to each boy, with no communication between them. The Shane part had been in operation earlier and now the Jon part had taken over with a vengeance, plunging her into a quagmire of panic and shame. She felt weak with worry. Her loyalty to Jon was too strong to enable her to make an excuse and wriggle out of their arrangement; anyway, she didn't want to. She loved snuggling up to him in a dark cinema, and sharing her thoughts about the movie with him later over a burger and a Coke. Yet at the same time she was dying to see Shane's flat and feel that excited fizz inside her which his nearness caused.

She sighed heavily, knowing there was only one thing to do ... and that was to leave it to Fate to sort it out. Once she'd decided on that, the heavy weight of responsibility fell off her. It would work out somehow. It *had* to.

Marsden End was a suburb of Marshdale. Viv had never been there and didn't know what to expect. She got off at the stop after the railway bridge, as Shane had directed, and found herself walking past a large redbrick wall, scarred with graffiti. The pavements were littered and dirty. Although it was a cold, windy day, a gang of small, noisy children were playing on the pavements in front of a row of tall Victorian houses whose window-sills were crumbling and whose window-frames hadn't seen a coat of paint for years.

Number 59 wasn't as bad as some of the others. The door was painted vivid green and there was a straggly, frostbitten conifer in a plastic tub at the top of the steps and window-boxes full of last year's dead plants on the sills. Obviously someone in the house had tried to make it look nice. Shane...?

Viv rang the bell. She couldn't hear a sound so she rang again, then knocked as directed. She was rewarded with the sound of footsteps thundering down a wooden staircase and the door was flung open to reveal Shane, in a navy Guernsey sweater and jeans and a pair of thick speckly wool socks, no shoes.

The hall was uncarpeted, like the stairs. Someone had made an attempt at stripping the wood on the banisters but hadn't finished the job, so patches of paint still clung to it. It was cold on the stairs – so cold that Viv could see her breath. Huge, bright canvases hung in the hallway and up the stairs, abstracts in oils, cheering up the freezing space.

"Who's the artist?" asked Viv, interested.

"Oh, that's Jane. She lives on the ground floor."

Shane's flat was on the first floor. As he flung open the door, a gust of welcoming warm air enveloped her. She clawed at the tightly fastened neck of her navy coat and undid it as quickly as she could.

"Phew!" she exclaimed when her coat was off.

Shane smiled proudly. "I've been warming the place up for you all day. I've got the heating on full blast. Coffee?"

He hung her coat on a wooden coatstand, painted scarlet. Guitar cases and amplifiers were stacked against the walls.

Shane led the way into his living room. It had high ceilings and huge windows which overlooked the street. The room was furnished with a huge sofa, draped in a turquoise, purple and red Indian cover, an armchair piled with multi-coloured cushions, a big old cupboard painted in marble-effect paintwork in pale blue, and an assortment of rugs and pictures. There were some big, leafy plants in pots. The walls were a pale sunshine yellow. The effect was one of warmth and lively energy.

"Do you like it?" Shane asked.

Viv sank into the armchair, the springs of which made a rude noise beneath her. She giggled nervously.

"That's the whoopee chair which I keep especially for guests," he joked. How nice of him to put her at her ease like that, rather than leave her writhing in embarrassment.

"You're certainly into colours, aren't you?" she observed.

"Jane says that different colours have different effects on your psyche. Purple is calming. Yellow is inspiring. Red is energy and activity and most of the blue shades are healing. That's why so many old medicine bottles used to be made of blue glass."

"Really?" Viv was fascinated. She followed Shane into the kitchen.

"'Scuse the mess," he apologized. It *was* a bit messy. Dirty crockery was mixed up with clean items left out to drain. A pan full of water sat in the sink. Cereal packets and biscuit packets were littering the work surface beneath the shabby old wooden cupboards. A soot-streaked gas heater hung above the sink. As Shane turned on the hot tap to rinse a mug, it erupted with a bang and a roar that made her jump.

"It's a bit temperamental, I'm afraid. Like me." He grinned as he lit the gas ring with a match taken from an enormous box.

"How long have you lived here?" Viv enquired, drifting curiously to the draughty sash window and looking out.

A shaft of lemon-coloured wintry sun shone through the branches of a giant horse-chestnut tree at the end of the garden and came to rest on a sad jungle of grass and dead weeds. But close to the window were the shiny, dark green leaves and scarlet berries of a flourishing holly tree. Viv could have reached out and plucked a sprig.

"Since last summer. The garden's great in summer. The cats can play hide and seek in it and it's a mass of wild flowers. Jane believes in leaving it as a wildlife area. You should see all the butterflies!" enthused Shane.

Who was this Jane she was hearing so much about? wondered Viv. An ex-girlfriend, perhaps? Or was there still something going on between them? She made a mental note to remember everything Shane said about her in case it gave her any clues.

"Sugar?" The coffee was ready.

"One, please," Viv told him.

They took their coffee and a packet of ginger biscuits back into the living room. Shane poked a CD into the machine. Viv was glad it was Simply Red and not Aerosmith or Megadeth. She sank into the depths of the armchair, then moved forward and sat poised on the edge of the seat. She couldn't settle, she was too tense, this was all too new and exciting.

Had things ever been like this in the beginning with Jon? She couldn't remember, it was too long ago. But no, it couldn't have been, she reasoned. They were much younger then and they lived at home with their parents. Jon's bedroom was the same now as it had been two years ago, the same Airfix models of tanks and planes, the same football posters.

This was the very first time she had ever been alone with a boy in a flat!

"Come and sit over here," said Shane, patting the sofa next to him. "The springs are broken in that chair."

Getting out of the armchair with a lurch, Viv knocked over her mug of coffee which had been balanced on the arm of the chair. Her hand flew to her mouth. "Oh dear, I'm really sorry," she said, blushing crimson in embarrassment at her clumsiness. Coffee stains were spreading on the armchair cover and on the rug the chair was standing on.

"Don't worry," Shane said, strolling into the kitchen and coming back with a wet dish sponge.

"Let me." Viv made a grab for the sponge and Shane's hand closed on her wrist.

"Relax!" he laughed. "You're like a little scurrying animal. I don't make you nervous, do I?"

"A bit," she admitted.

"Well, there's no need to be. I'm just a human being. A pretty scruffy one!"

A wave of affection for him rose like a lump in her throat and she smiled, meeting his vivid eyes. He smiled back, and there was a moment's silence between them that was so intimate that she could almost see the electricity dancing between them like golden lightning.

Then he looked away, bent down, finished mopping up and returned to the sofa. They had just started talking again when Shane said, "Oh look, you've got coffee on your sweatshirt."

Viv looked down and sure enough, there were splashmarks on her blue sweatshirt. And on her jeans. Damn!

Shane leapt up and returned with the sponge again. "Here you are – you'd better do it," he said, holding out the sponge to Viv.

As she took it from him, their fingers touched and she gave a jump as if she'd touched a live wire.

"Good job it's warm in here and it'll soon dry," she said, speaking too fast, almost gabbling with nerves.

Shane's eyes swept hers. There was a look in them that took her breath away.

"There is another way I can think of to help it dry quickly..." he murmured.

6

Shane put an arm round Viv's waist and drew her to him. As her body touched his, she sighed and felt herself relax against him, her body floppy and unresisting.

I shouldn't let him do this ... I should push him off. But it's heaven! I shouldn't be enjoying it ... Jon. Oh, help! If he kisses me now, I'll be lost! How will I be able to kiss Jon later with Shane's kisses still on my lips? Jon, Jon, walk through the door now and carry me off, don't let this happen to me. Protect me the way you've always done. *Don't let this happen!* wailed her anguished thoughts.

But it *was* happening, and she knew, while despising herself for it, that she wanted it to. Shane buried his mouth in the hair on the top of her head, kissing it, then moved his lips down to her forehead, and down, in a line of nibbly, pecky little kisses, over her temples, down the side of her face, around her ears, down her neck to the hollow of her collarbone.

"Stop it!" she laughed, pushing his face away. "It tickles."

So he started kissing her lips again and the rasp of his stubble against her chin sent little trickly shivers down her spine.

"You're a good kisser, Viv," he told her when they broke off for air.

"Years of practice," she told him airily, straightening her dark curls with a sweep of her hand.

"Oh!" he sounded surprised, as if he hadn't realized that she was only joking. "Have you had a lot of boyfriends, then?"

"No, I was joking. One or two very casual ones, and then Jon, for ages."

There – she'd actually spoken his name out loud! Would he forgive her? Fancy doing that! It was like bringing Jon to life in Shane's territory, seeing him standing there on the rug, with his sleek, neat, dark good looks, wearing the horn-rim specs he always wore for poring over his books.

How his face would darken in disbelief if he saw her like this, all dishevelled on the sofa next to Shane! What if he'd felt a vibe that she was up to no good? She'd read that people in love were sometimes quite telepathic with each other – not that she'd ever been able to read his mind or anything. But you never knew...

Shane must have felt her tense up, because he loosened his hold on her and moved away slightly.

"Do you want to tell me about him?" he asked.

"No," Viv said emphatically. "Why don't you tell me about you instead?"

"Well ... yes, I've had girlfriends, of course I

have. There've been quite a few since I was four-
teen. I'm nineteen now, I'll be twenty in May."

"Has there been ... anyone special?" Viv asked,
not sure if she wanted to know the answer.

"There were one or two I thought were special at
the time. But afterwards I wasn't so sure."

Then Viv asked the question she'd been dying to
ask. "Did you ever go out with Jane downstairs?"

Shane roared with laughter. "Jane? Good grief,
no! She's a great friend but – well, when you see
her you'll realize."

Viv had to be content with the mystery for now.

"Let me play something to you." Shane got up
and fetched the guitar, then sat cross-legged on
the rug with it. He began to strum. "Can you pass
me that sheet of paper? The one on top?" he asked
Viv.

She handed it to him and he placed it on the rug
in front of him.

"I've only just started writing this one. It's by no
means finished yet." The look on his face was a bit
guarded and apologetic, and almost shy.

> "Love is a fragile thing,
> Butterfly's wing,
> You can't hold it in your hand.
> A magic carpet flight
> Fast through the night
> To a city in the sand...
>
> Mirage, you don't exist,
> You're a trick of the summer mist,
> Oooh ... just a mirage of you."

"I haven't finished it yet," he said. "It's called *Mirage*."

"I gathered that," smiled Viv. Her heart was bumping in her chest. Is this song about me? she wondered. No, it can't be, he hasn't known me long enough to fall in love with me.

Shane was singing again, softly, huskily, sexily. His voice brought Viv out in goose-bumps. It was as if his song were bypassing her ears and going directly to her heart.

> *"You caught me off my guard.*
> *I tried very hard*
> *But I don't believe you're here.*
> *I'm scared to get too close,*
> *Find you're a ghost*
> *And watch you disappear..."*

He glanced up at Viv as he sang the last three lines, searching her eyes for something. She smiled and that seemed to do. He put the guitar down.

"You won't, will you?" he asked quietly.

"Won't what?" Her heart was thumping so rapidly, it was making her whole body vibrate.

"Disappear."

Viv didn't reply right away. She couldn't. She sat suspended in the silent romance of the moment. Nobody had written anything about her before. Jon had never written her a love letter or a poem, though she'd had cards from him with *All my love, Jon XXX* written on them.

That wasn't the same, though. This song had

taken a creative effort. She, plain Viv McCulloch, had been the inspiration for it. Somebody had felt enough about her to compose a work of art. Perhaps it would be a hit and the press would interview Shane and he'd tell the whole world that she had inspired it!

He was still waiting. What could she say? How could she make promises that she didn't know if she could keep? It was too soon ... too soon.

She shook her head, not daring to reply in words.

He smiled gently and kissed her again, on the cheek this time. Then he picked up the guitar once more and started to sing. He played some songs that Viv knew and joined in with. She surprised herself by being able to keep the tune going while he sang a harmony to it. At this rate, she mused, perhaps she'd end up in the group with him, as a backing singer! It was a thrilling thought...

After a long time, she remembered to look at her watch. It was nearly five o'clock and Jon was meeting her at the cinema at six.

"I'm sorry, I've got to go!" she said, standing up hastily.

Shane looked perplexed. "But I thought—"

"Thought what?"

He shrugged. "I don't know. Just thought we might do something, that's all."

"Like what?" Viv asked, intrigued.

"Um ... go to the cinema or something. There's a good movie on at the Cannon in Oldfield."

The Cannon! That's where she and Jon were going!

"Well?" Shane was waiting for a reply.

Viv gathered her scattered wits. "I can't. When you said come round this afternoon, I thought you meant you were busy this evening, so I've arranged to do something with a ... a friend."

He didn't notice her slight hesitation, thank goodness. What would he have thought of her if he'd known how glibly the fib had slid off her tongue?

"That's a pity. Still, it was my fault. How are you fixed during the week?"

Viv wished she had brought her diary with her. She frantically racked her brains. Tuesday was the night Jon usually had a meeting of a club he went to at school. She suggested that evening but Shane shook his head. "Got to help my cousin that night, I'm afraid. Do a spot of deejaying. How about Wednesday? Oh, no, damn, I've just remembered ... I've got a gig. Thursday?"

Viv couldn't for the life of her think as far ahead as Thursday, so she agreed to meet him then. It seemed an awfully long time away.

Shane asked if she minded getting the bus home as his van wasn't working. "I've got to take it in to the garage tomorrow," he said.

Viv was glad it was still early. She wouldn't have liked to be getting the bus home on her own at eleven o'clock. Shane kissed her at the door.

"See you Thursday, then. Shall I come and pick you up?" he offered.

"No, I'll meet you somewhere," Viv said quickly.

Shane asked for her phone number. There was nothing she wanted more than for him to call her, she thought as she wrote it down. But how would she explain who he was to her parents? She would have to think of another lie. Oh, dear ... she was getting into deeper and deeper water all the time.

They decided to meet outside one of the shops in the high street.

"Look after yourself. Sorry I can't come to the bus stop with you, I'm waiting for a phone call from one of the band. Oh, hi, Jane! This is Viv."

The woman who squeezed past Shane in the doorway was easily her mother's age and her large frame was clad in a huge, baggy, paint-splashed denim shirt and motheaten, faded black leggings. Her short hair was streaked with grey.

"Hello, I won't shake your hand, I've got turps all over it," Jane said, giving Viv a jolly smile.

"I love your paintings," Viv offered.

"Good. Then you must come to my next exhibition. I'll give Shane the details."

She thinks we're a couple, mused Viv as she waited at the bus stop, her scarf wrapped round her head and face to protect her ears from the biting wind. Do we look like one? She tried to picture herself and Shane standing together, he so tall and fair with his arm round her, and she with her dark curly head resting against his shoulder. She placed a blue sky behind them, dressed them in summer clothes, pictured Shane with a suntan and herself with her usual freckly nose.

Then she repeated the exercise with herself and Jon. That was easier because she had photographs of the two of them together. But the mental game didn't tell her anything. Two dark heads together looked just as good as a dark one and a blond one.

Jonathan Hammond, Shane Russell. Viv Hammond ... Viv Russell. Hmmm. She pictured herself in a church vestry signing the marriage register, but before she could decide which surname she was signing in it, the bus came.

7

Viv passed Trish a note during French. *Need urgent meeting in Mozart after school.* The Café Mozart did a great cappuccino and Viv felt greatly in need of one after the second half of last night. She felt even more urgently in need of some advice – which was why, after lengthy deliberation, she had decided to tell Trish everything that had been going on. It was only fair. Trish *was* her best friend, after all. She'd never have forgiven Viv if she'd heard the news through someone else.

The only table available was right next to one where some people she knew from school were seated.

"We can't sit there," she insisted. "Let's wait a bit."

"Oh, come on, Viv, what's wrong with that table? We'll be here all night at this rate – you know how popular this place is at this time of day," Trish grumbled.

"I have my reasons," Viv informed her mysteriously.

"They'd better be good ones. I've got my tap class tonight and I don't want to be late."

"Oh, look – I think those two are just going," observed Viv, ready to swoop on the table where two elderly ladies appeared to be fiddling with purses, handbags and umbrellas.

"Yes, girls, you can have our table in a minute, we're just going," one of them said, giving Viv a sweet smile.

Viv smiled back, inwardly willing them to hurry.

At last they were seated and the waitress had taken their order of two cappuccinos and a piece of gooey chocolate cake for Trish, whose sweet tooth never could resist temptation.

Trish leaned forward over the table. "Well, come on, then," she urged Viv. "What's this big secret all about?"

Viv bit her lip, knowing that she'd be in for it for deceiving her best friend.

"Um … you know how I promised I'd tell you everything that happened at Fiona's party?" she said, screwing her face into an exaggerated grimace in the hope of lightening the atmosphere and lessening Trish's anger. "Well, I didn't."

Trish looked blank. "What did you forget?" she asked, loosening her scarf and undoing the top two buttons of her school mac.

"I'm not sure how to tell you…"

"Oh, for heaven's sake, Viv, it can't be that bad!" Trish exclaimed. She took a huge, breathy slurp at the froth on the top of her coffee, then cut a wodge off her chocolate cake with a fork.

"It is," said Viv.

"Spit it out, then," said Trish, conveying the chunk of cake towards her lips.

"I ... met someone."

"You *what*?" Trish spluttered, blowing crumbs off her cake. "What do you mean, you met someone? You mean, like, a bloke, a male of the species, a fella?"

"Exactly that."

Trish shoved the cake into her mouth and started chomping so fast and mechanically that she couldn't have been tasting it at all. "But ... but I thought you went with Jon?" she asked as soon as her mouth was empty.

"I did go with Jon."

"Then how on earth did you manage to chat up someone else?"

"It wasn't quite like that..." Viv proceeded to tell Trish exactly what had taken place that evening, and on subsequent evenings, and all the time she was listening, Trish kept shovelling cake into her mouth like a robot and chewing and swallowing, her eyes round with scandalized excitement.

"... And then I had a big row with Jon because I didn't get to the cinema until after the film had started. And *then* I had to tell him I couldn't see him on Thursday. I'm sure he must be getting suspicious," she concluded dramatically. "So what do you think?"

"What I want to know is why you didn't tell me about all this sooner. I *am* supposed to be your best friend, after all," Trish said in an aggrieved tone. "You haven't told anyone else, have you? Rosie, for instance?"

"No. Why should I tell Rosie if I haven't told you?"

"Maybe you were scared of telling me because you know I'll give you an honest opinion and be tough with you if I think you deserve it," Trish said. It was true. She was notoriously outspoken and blunt, but had rarely had cause to get heavy with Viv. Yet.

"Look, I *am* sorry I didn't tell you sooner, but you can imagine how I felt," Viv said beseechingly. "I didn't expect anyone to approve of my behaviour exactly, least of all you. I don't even approve of it myself!"

"So why go behind Jon's back like this? Why don't you simply tell him you want to start seeing someone else?"

"Because it's not as straightforward as that." Viv raked agitated fingers through her hair. "Oh, I know you won't believe me, Trish, but I still love Jon. All the things I ever felt for him, I still feel. It's still a thrill to be close to him, it's still great when we go out together. I haven't gone off him at all, so how can I finish with him? I don't *want* to."

Viv pressed her hands over her eyes for a moment. She felt as if she was on trial. Trish was sitting there, looking so accusing and critical, waiting for her to explain her awful behaviour, and how could she, when she couldn't even explain it to herself?

She removed her hands and raised her eyebrows and gazed despairingly at her friend.

"I know I'm behaving badly but I can't stop," she said, "and you know why? It's because they're both really gorgeous, both really nice and I'm equally drawn to both of them, for different reasons. It's hopeless," Viv sighed. "I don't expect you to understand. I don't expect *anyone* to."

"So you're going to carry on stringing both of them along? Honestly, Viv, I didn't think you were that type. It seems you just want to have your cake and eat it."

Trish was getting heated and Viv sneaked a look round the café, to ensure nobody could hear her raised voice. "Ssh!" she hissed warningly, but Trish went on.

"It's not fair on either of them, you know. Most of us would be glad of *one* nice, good-looking boyfriend, but you seem to be hogging the whole supply!"

"It's not like that," said Viv defensively.

"You must like one of them more than the other, surely?"

"That's the trouble." Viv sighed deeply and rested her elbows on the table, plonking her chin in her cupped hands. "I've spent sleepless nights thinking about it and I do like them both, but for different reasons. They're exact opposites, and I'm somewhere stuck in the middle."

"Well, you can't carry on like this, because it's only a matter of time before you get found out. I know! Remember last year when I started seeing Mike before I'd finished with Robbie?" Trish reminded her. "Then I accidentally double-booked myself and they both came round on the same evening? I'll never forget the things Robbie said to me, the names he called me. And he was quite right. He was so hurt, Viv. I don't think Jon deserves that treatment. You really ought to have the guts to finish with him."

"But I've *told* you. I don't *want* to finish with him!" Viv wailed. "I still love him."

"Do you love Shane?"

Viv laughed out loud. "For heaven's sake, Trish, I've only just met him!" Then she hesitated, finally saying, slowly and thoughtfully, "I don't know if that matters, though. You see, the moment I saw him, I felt as though I'd fallen madly in love with him. It's crazy! Jon and I were friends before we started going out together. We fell in love after that. But this is the other way round. I've never known anything like it. It's quite scary, really."

"Maybe you love Jon but you're *in* love with Shane," Trish suggested.

Viv thought about that in silence for a moment, then burst out with, "Oh, Trish, I do wish you'd been at Fiona's party, then you'd have seen him for yourself. He's just ... oh, I don't know. He's got something. Some kind of special aura about him. He's different. You know how practical Jon is? Well, Shane's poetic, he writes songs. He's even written one about me! Can you imagine Jon ever doing anything like that?"

"Jon's thoughtful, though. He sends you cards even if he doesn't make up the rhymes himself. That shows he's got a romantic side," Trish pointed out. "What kind of Valentine cards do you think they'll both send you?"

Valentine's Day! She hadn't even thought about

it! It wasn't that long off. Just over two weeks...

Her mind raced ahead. What if Jon took her out for a romantic meal and asked her to get engaged to him before he went off to college in the autumn? Or would he take her to the school Valentine's dance? What if *Shane* wanted to take her out that night?

Trish snapped her fingers in Viv's face. "Wake up! I shall count from ten to one and when I say one, you will..."

Viv laughed at Trish's hypnotist impression. "Sorry, I was just thinking about Valentine's Day."

"You said you wanted my advice?" Trish leant forward over the table, bringing her auburn head very close to Viv's. "Stick to Jon. He's the best you'll ever hope to find. He's clever, he's hard-working, he's ambitious, he's handsome, he's kind, he's thoughtful—"

"Sounds as though you're in love with him yourself," commented Viv, interrupting this flow of praise.

"Don't be stupid," responded Trish. "Anyway, I've got Mike. Look, this is what I always do when I can't make up my mind about something. Here's a piece of paper – " she pushed a paper napkin across the table – "and here's a pen. Write both their names at the top and a plus and minus column of their good and bad points under each. Bet there'll be more pluses under Jon's name and more minuses under Shane's."

"I'll try it," Viv promised. "I'll do it at home, not here." She didn't want to do it at all. Whoever failed the test, she would just end up even more confused and she didn't think she could cope with that. If only fate would suddenly step in and tell her what to do. If something could happen to remove one of them from the scene, she wouldn't have to make a choice.

"No, God, I didn't mean *that* sort of removal!" she told her bedroom ceiling later that evening. "I don't want either of them to die or anything!" But maybe a rich uncle in Australia could invite Jon to spend a year on his ranch ... or perhaps Shane's band could be offered a lengthy tour of Europe. If fate would remove either boy, just for a while, it would make her life so much easier, without her having to make any decisions. She knew that was a wimpish way out of her problem, but right now it seemed the only way.

Yet, if either of them were to vanish from her life, she'd miss him dreadfully. Life without Jon ... it was unthinkable. Those kind brown eyes that could suddenly sparkle in fun, that serious frown, that quick, warm smile; the firm, dry, strong hand in hers, his arm round her, so companionable, so protective; nestling against his tall, hard body, her head against his shoulder; all the things they had shared over two long, love-filled years... No, there would be a huge gap in her heart, part of her would be missing, if he went. The pain of his absence would be awful.

But if *Shane* were suddenly to disappear... Oh, the pain of that, too! She felt a sharp pang in her midriff and clutched her arms tightly around herself under the bedcovers. Not to see that dazzling, teasing smile ever again, or feel the intense radiance of those penetrating blue eyes. Never again to feel the excitement of his lips touching hers, involving her in a kiss that set her heart leaping and her whole body quivering with passion. Having to miss for ever the sound of his voice, the lilt of his guitar strings, the sheer poetry of his songs, the heart-grabbing romance of those words written specially for her. He loved her, she knew he did.

But Jon loves me too. And me ... who do I love? Viv felt that no girl before her had ever been in such distress and felt so torn and mean and unfair and mixed up. Every day she kept telling herself to stop seeing Shane. He was the new-comer, her relationship with Jon was two years old, there should be no choice between them. But the trouble was, every time she was out with Jon, it felt like he was the only man in her life, and that they were a couple and Shane didn't exist. And every time she was out with Shane, it was *Jon* who didn't exist.

What's wrong with me? Am I a schizophrenic? she wondered. It felt as if her brain and her heart were split into two and each part could operate independently of the other one.

I'm crazy, she told herself. I'm utterly mad. If not, then I'm going insane and I soon will be.

One of the things helping to drive her mad was the strain of always having to remember what she had said to which boy. She felt as devious as a spy as she carefully searched her memory to make sure that she wasn't about to refer to something she'd done with Shane when she was with Jon, and vice versa. Once or twice there had been near misses, but she'd stopped herself just in time as the consequences of being found out just didn't bear thinking about.

With Valentine's Day approaching, she was put in even more of a spin. She felt so ashamed of herself that she bought them cards in separate shops in case the woman at the till thought she was a terrible person for buying two.

The cards she got were completely different. Jon's had a cute yellow teddy-bear on the front, clutching its heart – he had given her a teddy soon after they had started going out and bears were a personal symbol of theirs – and the words, *Valentine, I can't BEAR to be without you* written inside. She wrote, *Geddit? It's true. From U-know-Who! XXXX*. As she scribbled the message, she felt terrible, as if her very writing was exposing her as the phoney she really was.

For Shane, she searched far and wide for a card connected to music, putting far more care and effort into choosing it than she had with Jon's. In the end, she settled on a reproduction of a painting of a girl in medieval costume and long, shining hair, playing a kind of guitar. The card was blank inside and she wrote that famous quotation from Shakespeare, *If music be the food of love, play on*. He would guess who it was from – she hoped!

8

On Tuesday evening, Viv took the bus across town after school to meet Shane from college. He had told her that his last lecture would be over by five.

It was sleeting and she sheltered in the college doorway, not liking to go in because of the rather forbidding interior and the grim-faced man at the reception desk.

As she stood huddled against the brickwork, with her school scarf, which was a distinctive red and blue, wrapped around her neck and face, she saw Jon. He was on the top deck of a bus and the traffic was crawling along due to the appalling weather. He was staring out of the window and seemed to be looking right at her. She turned her head away and flattened herself against the corner of the glass door, trying to pretend she wasn't really there.

Her scarf would have caught his eye, she felt sure. What on earth was she going to say if he asked her what she was doing there? She would have to think of an alibi.

What if he got off at the next stop and came back? She'd told him she was staying in to do some work tonight so he'd be bound to be curious. In desperation, she pushed open the door of the college and went in. There was no safe place to hide in the entrance hall, so she steeled herself to walk past the desk. The man glanced briefly at her, but said nothing as she walked past him to the lifts.

Shane had mentioned a students' bar. She could hang around in there for a while and come back down in ten minutes or so, by which time Jon, if he had decided to look for her, would have given up. A lift came and as she was about to step into it, she saw Shane about to get out. He looked surprised to see her.

"I was a bit early so I thought I'd get a drink at the bar as it's so cold," she invented rapidly.

"What a great idea!" he said, and hauled her back into the lift, and safety.

They had a lovely evening. After the college bar, they went to a vegetarian restaurant where a man was playing the piano and singing. She never seemed to discover places like that when she was with Jon. With Shane, she felt like a tourist in her own town. Their time together felt like a holiday, something outside of real life. A treat, an adventure, a miracle. And what was even more magical was that all through their date, there was the tingling anticipation of how the evening would end, with Shane's arms round her and his lips touching hers, filling her with such incredible, hardly bearable, blissful feelings.

When she got home, her mother told her that Jon had rung.

"Oh, I won't ring him back now, it's a bit late," she said.

"Do I detect a slight cooling off in the air?" asked her mother.

Viv tried to stem a blush as she answered, "No, what makes you think that?"

Her mother ignored her and pressed on. "Could it possibly be connected to a certain boy called Shane who's rung you once or twice?"

"Shane's just a friend. Anyway, it's none of your business," Viv pointed out huffily. She began to go up the stairs to her room.

"True," her mother replied, "but you can hardly blame me for being interested."

"Mum, I can assure you that if I'm about to make any big changes in my life, you'll be one of the first to hear," Viv called down from the top of the stairs. "Good night!"

Why had Jon rung her? The question plagued her until well after midnight. He must have seen her. If not, she'd had a very close call.

Next morning, she opened her curtains to find that the garden was inches deep in snow. That was the first surprise of the day. The second was a phone call from Jon while she was eating breakfast, during which he made no mention of having seen her the previous evening.

He wanted to know what her plans for Saturday were as one of the guys from the sixth form college which Jon attended was having a party. Viv said she'd love to go. He also said she had to keep a week on Tuesday free. That, Viv realized with a flutter of dread in her heart, was Valentine's Day...

There's a saying that things always happen in threes – and indeed Fate had a third surprise in store because, as Viv was scrunching through the snow towards the school gates with Trish and Rosie that afternoon, who should be standing leaning against the side of his van in the snowy gloom, but Shane.

"Oh!" Viv exclaimed, her gloved hand flying to her mouth.

"Who's that?" asked Rosie.

"That's not *him*, is it?" asked Trish.

"Who's 'him'?" enquired Rosie, who had not yet been let in on the secret.

"Viv's latest boyfriend," Trish enlightened her.

Rosie's face was a study. "I don't know anything about this," she began.

Viv's mind had already crossed the distance that her feet ached to run. "It's a long story. Trish can fill you in," she said, and set off walking as quickly as she could on snow that had been trampled into slippery ice.

"Hi," she said shyly, thinking how gorgeous he looked in a leather flying jacket with the fleecy collar pulled up to his ears. His blond hair was blurred with snowflakes. He must have been standing there for some time, waiting for her. A rush of warm gratitude filled her. And pride. He was by far the best looking guy who had ever stood by the school gates waiting for anyone. She wouldn't have been surprised to find movie cameras lurking on the far side of the street.

"It was such a dreadful day that I thought you'd be glad of a lift home," he said cheerfully. "Can't have my girl getting chilblains, can I?"

She flashed him a grateful smile, but his words had given her a jolt. "My girl," he'd called her. But she was Jon's girl...

If she was Jon's girl, though, what on earth was she doing in the van with Shane?

She loved driving with him because it gave her a chance to study his profile. His nose had a sexy bump on the bridge. There was a scar on his top lip which he'd collected playing football as a kid, which gave him a slight tough-guy look which added to his attractiveness. He'd told her how heartbroken his mother had been when the doctor had told her her blond-haired angel might be scarred for life.

"I told her that when I was a big person, I'd grow a beard and moustache and hide it," he said. "I think she was even more horrified at the thought of that than she was about the scar!"

His chin stuck out exactly far enough and it had a tiny cleft in it, like a dimple, beneath his bottom lip. He was wearing a different earring today, she noticed, in the shape of a tiny silver guitar. She resisted a sudden urge to reach over and touch the shining metal ornament with her tongue.

"Do you want to go straight home?" he asked.

"I've got to. It's homework night. I've got to stay in and swot for a test tomorrow."

"I suppose there's no point in hoping that you might ask me in to sit and drink coffee while you work?"

This was just what she had been dreading! How could she ever invite Shane in, with her nosy parents around, as well as the chance that Jon might drop in unexpectedly, or ring her up and want a long chat?

"Er ... we're in chaos at home at the moment. Mum doesn't want visitors because Dad's in the middle of decorating."

Viv was quite horrified at the way the rapid invention tripped so easily off her tongue. She hated herself for lying, but what else could she do? There was no way she could invite Shane home and run the gamut of a parental interrogation – and what if Jon should come round? He often dropped in out of the blue after school, and stayed for a coffee and some of Viv's mother's fantastic home-made cheesy biscuits, which he adored.

"I could always offer him a hand. I've done quite a bit of decorating," Shane said brightly. Viv tensed, her hands balled into fists. She could hardly breathe, she was so scared. It seemed Shane was determined to come in at all costs. She had to think of something.

They were nearing her road now. She put her hand on his knee. "Shane, I'm really sorry. I've got a lot of homework to do tonight. There's no way I can get out of it. Will you forgive me?" she begged him.

"Of course I will," he said.

The nearside tyres of the van bumped over a pile of snow which someone had cleared off the pavement, as he parked close to her house. He put his arm round her. Viv's heart was thumping from a mixture of his nearness, the scent of his sexy cologne, and her guilty fear that Jon might walk up the street at any moment. It was unlikely, especially in this weather, but you just never knew...

It was dark and the street light outside her house wasn't working, fortunately. Viv surrendered herself to Shane's kiss which, even in this tense and anxious moment, still worked its magic.

"Are you *sure* you have to go in?" Shane groaned. "You know, girls who kiss like you should have Government Health Warnings stamped on your foreheads. You could give even the healthiest of men a heart attack!"

Viv laughed with him. "See you really soon," she said, lifting her heavy briefcase full of books off the van's rusty, dusty floor.

"Well, the weekend's no good, unless you want to come to Aylesbury! We're doing someone's wedding bash on Saturday night, then one of the guys has found a studio for us to rehearse in. We can have it all Sunday and every evening next week."

"Oh." Viv's face fell.

Shane grinned. "Do you honestly think I can go a whole week without seeing you?" he said. "I'll wriggle out of a rehearsal as soon as I can. And by the way," he added, as Viv was preparing to slam the van door shut after climbing out, "don't fix up anything for Tuesday week, will you? I've got tickets to a special Valentine's Day do. I hope you don't get seasick!"

9

"*Oh, no ... oh, NO! What am I going to DO?*"
Viv sat on her bed with her hands over her ears, shaking her head from side to side. She seemed to hear two bells ringing, one in either ear. But instead of going *ding-dong*, they were going *Shane-Jon ... Shane-Jon*. She was going to have to choose. But which one?

Jon had phoned her and told her that he was going to take her out for a special Valentine's meal. "Wear that gorgeous red dress," he had requested, in the tender, intimate, loving tone that made her arms go all goose-bumpy. "I really fancy you in it."

"All right," she'd agreed, hearing her voice go all low and throaty. "Where are you taking me?"

"It's a secret," he had said.

Shane's Valentine destination wasn't a secret – he wanted to take her to a disco on a boat!

"It starts at eight-thirty and goes on till one," he'd told her. "The music will be great – it's my friend doing the disco again, the one who did the music for your friend's party – and the food and two free drinks are included in the price of the ticket. Not that it's going to cost *you* anything," he'd added hastily. "It'll be a really good night."

It obviously didn't cross his mind that she might have other arrangements for the evening of Valentine's Day – and why should it? Both Shane and Jon thought they were the only boy in her life. How many other girls had more than one offer of a Valentine date? Viv wondered. She knew some girls would boast about it and think they were clever, but not her. Trish called her a two-timer, but she didn't think she was. Two-timers were shallow, heartless people, they were multiple-daters for the fun of it, they didn't care about the lies they told and the hearts they broke.

Real two-timers didn't suffer. But Viv did. She suffered nightmares of guilt every time she told a lie, and every time she came home from a date. How was it all going to end? And now she was faced with this latest dilemma!

Which date would I rather go on? she asked herself. Say I had the choice, and there was no problem of having to choose between partners involved...

Successive pictures floated across her mind's eye: she and Jon holding hands and gazing at each other across a small table, through the glow of a candle ... being held tightly against Shane's warm, strong body while her feet drifted through the movements of a slow, slow dance.

She had taken her hands away from her ears

74

now and was sitting on the edge of her bed, her arms dangling loosely and hopelessly by her sides. It was well past midnight and her parents had gone to bed ages ago. But for her, sleep was impossible. So was her dilemma...

How could she possibly turn down her steady boyfriend on Valentine's Day? It would be the end of her relationship. Unless she was actually lying in bed in hospital, he just wouldn't believe any excuse and would be terribly hurt. She simply couldn't do it to him. Poor Jon... He hadn't done a thing wrong. It was she who was in the wrong, entirely.

But how could she not accept Shane's invitation, especially when he had had to make a sacrifice to invite her?

"Steve asked me to help him with the disco but, even though I could have done with the money, I turned him down. I told him I had a beautiful partner for the evening who I wanted to spend every minute with," he had declared.

Viv had felt herself blush. Shane had a knack of making her feel special, and attractive. He had a way with words which Jon, for all his sincerity and depth of feeling, lacked. Whereas Shane might say, "Your hair looks like a piece of the midnight sky that somebody has cut out," Jon would merely remark, "Had your hair done, Fluffy-head?"

Yet, much as Shane's poetic language spoke to a deep vein of romance in her, Jon's use of a private nickname awoke feelings of familiarity and tenderness and security. She loved Jon's warm brown eyes, his teasing grin. She loved the way he made her feel loved. She didn't have that with Shane; not yet. Their relationship was far too new for her to be able to predict him, and trust him.

Thinking of Jon now gave her tugging feelings in her heart. She pictured him sitting at the desk in his bedroom, hunched over his textbooks, his brow rumpled above his glasses, chewing the end of a ballpoint pen. She wanted to step up behind him and knead his aching shoulders and rest her cheek in the safe haven of his friendly-smelling hair. He was part of her, and she of him.

So what exactly was she up to with Shane?

If Viv had had a pound for every time she'd tried to arrive at an answer to that question, she would be able to afford a holiday by now.

"I'm physically attracted to him, and fascinated by him because he's new and different, but it'll wear off," was one of the conclusions she'd come up with. But it didn't ring quite true. After several dates, she was feeling more for him, not less.

"Perhaps I wanted to know what it was like going out with somebody different..." But that wasn't right, either. She had been perfectly content with Jon until she'd encountered the force of those vivid blue eyes ... felt the heat of that summer-sun smile.

"Perhaps I'm going off Jon without realizing it, and this is my subconscious's way of telling me..." No, she wasn't going off Jon. She loved him as much as ever.

"Do I love Shane?" she wondered out loud. Well, her heart started bumping about every time she pictured his face. Whenever she picked up a paper or magazine, the name "Shane" seemed to leap off the page and hit her where her heart was. When she was on her way to meet him, she would go all jelly-legged and butterflies – no, they were more like eagles – would flap around in her stomach.

Had she felt that way when she'd first met Jon? She couldn't remember, it was too long ago. Anyway, she'd been a lot younger then and their romance had started off as a childhood friendship.

Her brain was going round and round in circles. Maybe it was time to do what Trish suggested and make a list! She tiptoed downstairs, tore a sheet of paper from the large pad her mother kept in the kitchen, and crept back upstairs. She rested the paper on a book on her bed and wrote *Jon* on the left-hand side and *Shane* on the right. Beneath both names she made two lists headed *Pros* and *Cons*.

Then she began...

Jon – Pros: He loves me; I trust him; He's faithful; Kind; Sensitive; Intelligent; Thoughtful; Interesting; Sexy; We really know each other.

The *Jon – Cons* list read: Works too hard; Broke (she felt mean having written that and promptly crossed it out); Going away in autumn; Too serious sometimes; Predictable.

She stopped and sucked the end of her pen thoughtfully. Had she omitted anything? She couldn't think of anything more so she started on the *Shane* list.

Shane – Pros: Gorgeous; Funny; Talented; Makes me feel good; Very sexy; Romantic.

Shane – Cons: She had to rack her brains and suck her pen some more, but finally she came up with "Haven't known him long". That was a "con" that time could cure. But then, time might also cure most of the points against Jon.

Suddenly, she yawned and felt monumentally tired. I'll read it all through in the morning and decide then, she told herself before switching out the light.

Next day, she took the list into school and appealed to Trish for help in making some sense of it. They worked on it in their lunchbreak, shivering in coats, hats, scarves and gloves in a corner of the yard.

"Jon's got ten Pros and Shane's only got six. Jon's the winner so far," announced Trish.

"But I could have pinched half Jon's list and given it to Shane. He's intelligent, sensitive and interesting, too!" Viv protested.

"But you didn't. Now let's look at the Cons. Five against Jon and only one against Shane. One? Are you being fair, Viv? The only reason why you can think more up for Jon is because you know him better. If you knew Shane better, you might write things like mean, moody, untrustworthy ... you just don't know."

"Look, I asked for help, Trish. Help! Not an anti-Shane campaign."

Trish scowled. "OK, OK. I'm only telling you how I see it. Maybe Shane really is God's gift to women like you seem to think. But if he's so wonderful, why doesn't he have hundreds of girls falling at his feet and following him everywhere?"

"Why doesn't Jon? You seem to think *he's* God's gift," Viv fired back, then added, "Are you trying to imply something here, like if Shane's so wonderful, what's he doing going out with me?"

"No, no," Trish said quickly. "Calm down." She put a hand on Viv's arm. "I'm biased, I'll admit it. I think Jon's great. Sometimes I think you don't know how lucky you are and take him for granted, that's all. I think you should forget Shane and stick with him. Boys like him don't grow on trees."

"How about boys like Shane?"

"Hmm," Trish said thoughtfully. "My old gran used to say that you shouldn't trust blokes who are too handsome." A gust of wind threatened to blow her woolly hat off and she clung to it. "Wretched thing. Wish I'd stuck some hairpins in it."

"Just a mo... I thought you said Jon was handsome," Viv pointed out. She wasn't in a mood to let Trish get away with anything. Not after she'd been so anti-Shane. "You said he looks like Hugh Grant!"

"He does, a bit," spoke a different voice. It was Rosie, coming over to join them. She rubbed her rainbow-mittened hands. "Brrr! I'm sure it's going to snow again. What's the score?"

"Jim-and-Tonic's off with flu so we've got a free period this afternoon, hooray!" Jim McConnich was their form teacher. He'd acquired his nickname after a rumour that he'd once got completely legless on gin and tonic at a staff party.

"No, stupid!" Rosie berated Trish. "Viv's score. The Jon versus Shane game."

"Just about a draw, I think," Viv said hastily.

"Looks like Fate's not going to make it easy for you. Why not try dip-dip-dip?" Rosie laughed.

"You unsympathetic brute! We're talking about people here – with *feelings*. Not sweets or cakes," snorted Viv.

Rosie slung an arm round her shoulders and gave her a hug. "Look," she said, "we don't mean it, we were just having a bit of a tease. We do think you're getting more than your fair share of luck in the boy department, but we know it's not easy for you. I certainly don't know what *I'd* do under the circumstances. I couldn't cope. You must be a lot stronger than me."

"Or me," Trish put in. "I don't think we're being very helpful. It's hard to know what advice to give. We know you're not being deliberately nasty to the guys. We wouldn't want to know you if you were. I suppose all we can say is, enjoy it for as long as you can, because the situation can't last for ever."

"I agree with Trish," Rosie said. "It's hard for us, though, because we like Jon and you two have been an item for so long that we can't imagine you with anyone else. Cheer up. Still friends?"

Viv swallowed hard, trying to remove the lump in her throat and gave them a wan grin. "Still friends."

10

February 12th arrived. "Made your mind up yet?" Rosie asked at school that day.

"No," wailed Viv.

The day seemed to drag on for ever and what she desperately needed was time to herself, to think. But at last she was alone in her bedroom, staring at the two envelopes she was going to post in the morning. She felt she truly knew the meaning of the expression, "paralysed by indecision".

February 13th came. She posted the cards. Would she get any tomorrow? she wondered. Then an awful thought struck her. What if both her boyfriends decided to deliver their cards in person and arrived at her door at the same time?

As for the fateful Valentine's evening, Jon had promised to come round for her at seven. Shane had asked her to meet him at the White Swan at eight-fifteen, because the boat was leaving at eight-thirty from the landing stage by the riverside pub. The only thing she could do was pray for the boat trip to be cancelled. But then Shane might come round to her house and find her out with Jon...

She passed a wretched night, tossing and turning and sleeping fitfully and having anxious dreams when she did. When her alarm went off at seven-thirty, she felt so exhausted that she contemplated telling the world she was ill and pulling the covers over her head and staying there till the 15th. That would solve all her problems!

"Viv!" her mother yelled up the stairs. "Something's arrived for you."

She dragged herself wearily out of bed and padded to the top of the stairs. Her mother was down in the hallway holding an exquisite bouquet of yellow roses and pink tulips in a florist's wrapper. "Your dad found them on the doorstep when he left for work," she explained.

"They must be from Jon," Viv said, praying that they were as she didn't want to have to answer any awkward questions.

Her mother brought them up to her and she retreated into her bedroom in order to read whatever message lay hidden inside the small white envelope which protruded from the pink satin bow round the stems of the flowers.

To my Valentine. I hope you're not just a mirage.
Shane! Her pulse raced as she cradled the card against her heart. She laid the bouquet on her dressing table and started to get dressed. She had one foot in her tights when she heard the sound of the doorbell, and then her mother's voice calling her again.

"Viv? *More* flowers for you! And some cards. You're very popular this year."

Her mother pushed open her door and thrust another bouquet at her, of red roses this time, then sent not one, or two, but *four* envelopes flying on to her bed.

"Don't spend too long opening them, it's a quarter past eight," said her mother warningly.

This bouquet was from Jon. *To my darling Fluffy-head. Forever your Valentine. All my fondest, soppiest love, Jon.* Just one X, but an enormous one.

She laid Jon's flowers on her bed and started to open her cards. The first one turned out to be Jon's. It was of the red padded satin heart variety. *To My Valentine* it said on the front and inside was a printed verse:

> *I love you more than words can say.*
> *My love grows stronger every day.*
> *Without your love I'd fade and pine.*
> *So say you'll stay forever mine.*

Underneath, with no attempt to disguise his writing, he'd put, *I love you. Jon*, then filled the bottom two inches of blank space with dozens of crosses.

She kissed the satin heart and laid the card gently down and attacked the next envelope. As she ripped it open and delved inside, she shrieked as an object on a spring leaped out at her, making a metallic squawking noise. When she'd got over the shock, she looked and saw it was a white plastic duck. *I'm quackers about you, Valentine*, it said inside the card. It was unsigned and there was no written message. It was a mystery.

So was the third card. It was drenched with a perfume which seemed familiar but she couldn't place it. There was a soppy looking dog on the front with *Be My Valentine* written below it. Inside, in scrawly, obviously disguised handwriting, it said, *To the Marchioness of Marshdale from one of her many admirers.*

What?

"Twenty to nine, Viv!" bellowed her mother. She didn't start work till ten, lucky thing.

"OK!" Viv yelled back. Then she opened the last card. It was beautiful. The picture on the front looked hand-painted and was a desert scene at sunset, but the sun was a heart coming over the horizon with a teeny camel silhouetted against it. Inside were some of the lines from Shane's *Mirage* song but, in true romantic Valentine fashion, he'd left it unsigned. Unlike Jon...

Viv hid all four cards in a drawer and dashed off to school. She was nearly there when she realized she'd forgotten to put her flowers in water.

Between lessons, she passed Rosie in the corridor. "How many cards did the Marchioness receive?" giggled Rosie.

"You beast!" shrieked Viv, getting a whiff of that perfume again and realizing it was *Rive Gauche* which someone had given Rosie for Christmas. "And I suppose a quacking duck that nearly hit me in the eye was nothing to do with you?"

"No, but it might have something to do with Trish," Rosie sniggered.

"I'll see to you two at lunchtime!" Viv threatened.

It turned out that the two extra cards had been sent with the best of intentions.

"You see, we thought that if you got lots, it would put Jon off the scent, whereas if you'd just got two..." Trish explained.

"I understand. Thanks," Viv said. "And *don't* ask me about tonight because I still don't know."

Her stomach felt in a dreadful state all afternoon. She hadn't eaten a crumb all day. As she smoothed the red dress down over her hips that evening, she felt so sick and looked so pale that she wouldn't have needed an excuse to wriggle out of any date.

She sank weakly down on to the edge of her bed. Shane's face swam before her eyes ... those heart-rendingly blue eyes, that smile that always began with twitches at the corner of his mouth and a dimple appearing in his chin, that stubborn stubble which was oh, so masculine when it grazed her face. Being with him was constant excitement always. She never knew what he was going to say, or where he was going to take her. He was an enigma.

Then, with a thrilling tingle, she recalled the scent of his skin, a masculine odour which was so different from Jon's. Half-closing her eyes, she relived that moment when Shane put his arm round her and drew her against him and his face darkened and his breathing quickened and his lips reached for hers, hard and crushing in their passion and need. At that moment, she was drawn into a secret, uncertain world, where danger, excitement and ecstasy lurked round every corner. She gave a shudder, feeling her body respond to the memory. She was hooked on it, she couldn't give it up. She couldn't wait till the next time she saw him, heard him, tasted him.

Then she visualized Jon's face, the amber-brown eyes that glowed like love-lanterns when he looked at her, the high cheekbones and clean angles of his face, the gleaming wing of dark hair which fell over his forehead, his lovely, teasing sense of humour, the way he was such a good friend always, standing by her and being sympathetic whatever her mood.

"Oh, God," she said out loud, meeting her reflection in the mirror, "there's nothing for it. Somehow, I'm going to have to go out with *both* of them tonight!"

11

Viv wasn't quite ready when Jon arrived, so her father invited him into the lounge to wait for her. When she eventually came downstairs, still feeling uneasy and preoccupied, he had come out of the lounge and was pacing up and down in the hall, looking at his watch.

"Sorry," she apologized. "My hair just wouldn't go right."

He grunted. "Looks all right to me. Come on, we're late." No sweet smile, no tender kiss, no slipping of his arm around her waist. What had happened to the romantic Valentine mood he should have been in? Viv wondered. As they walked down the street towards the bus stop, she got in close with her hip brushing against his, but, unusually, he didn't take her hand. She felt hurt ... bewildered.

He walked fast so that she had to trot to keep up. At the bus stop, she tucked her arm through his in the hope of creating some intimacy between them. He made no move to stop her, but neither did he give her arm a loving squeeze between his arm and his waist. With that rather stern look on his face as he gazed up the road in the direction from which the bus would come, he looked impossibly handsome.

Viv felt her heart give a jolt as she saw the shadow of his long, dark lashes cast on his cheekbone by the orange glow of the street lamp. Sometimes she experienced moments like this, when she suddenly saw Jon as if seeing him for the first time and was struck all over again by how utterly gorgeous he was, with that bony face of his, the determined angles of his jaw, the tall, proud stance. It was almost like falling in love with him all over again and she yearned for him to look her way, with eyes that beamed warmth and love at her and told her she was cherished and appreciated.

But tonight – Valentine's night – he didn't seem to be doing much cherishing. He didn't even help her on to the platform of the bus but forged ahead and up the stairs, leaving her to follow.

Once in the Thai restaurant which he had chosen as their Valentine venue, his manners improved a little. At least he pulled back the chair for her and waited until she had sat down before seating himself.

Viv found herself comparing this evening with a year ago, when he had taken her to a romantic Italian bistro where the waiters serenaded her and a girl with a basket of red roses came in and gave her a dozen luscious, crimson blooms. He had held her hand as much as possible during the meal, had stroked it tenderly, gazed deeply and soulfully into her eyes and had told her repeatedly how much he loved her. But tonight he hadn't said it once. It was almost as if they were just friends, rather than boyfriend and girlfriend.

Oh, Jon, Viv silently yearned. *Please tell me you love me. Please tell me everything's all right.*

Her stomach was churning with anxiety so that she could hardly eat any of the food, which, in any case, was too hot and spicy for her taste. *What if he's found out about Shane?* she fretted. But, if he had, he'd surely have cancelled this date.

Plucking up all her courage, she asked him, in a voice wavery with nerves, "Jon ... er ... what's wrong?"

He wouldn't answer at first. Instead, he scowled down at his plate, spearing a prawn with a furious stab of his fork.

Viv reached out and placed her hand on his free one. "Please tell me," she begged.

He looked up and there was pain in his dark eyes.

"I'll tell you what's wrong," he said, in a tight, angry voice. "It's seeing my roses – my special Valentine roses which were meant just for you and were really expensive – mixed up with a load of other flowers. I thought that you cared a bit more than that, Viv, that's all!"

"Oh, no! I had no idea!" Viv said, shocked. It was true. She hadn't set foot in the lounge all day. "I love you, Jon. I'd *never* do a thing like that, Jon, please believe me!"

She stared at him beseechingly. What a dreadful thing to have happened! Poor Jon, she could just imagine how he must have felt when he saw them. Tears stung her eyes as she put herself in his place.

"It must have been Mum," she said through compressed, angry lips. "Dad must have given her some flowers, too, and she tried to do something artistic with them all, without thinking. Oh, Jon, I *am* sorry! I'll tell her off as soon as I get home."

She leaned forward and seized his hand, giving it a squeeze. She felt truly penitent, even though the fib about the other flowers being her mother's tripped off her lips so easily that she almost believed it herself.

"You see," she elaborated, "I was late this morning and when they arrived I read the card that came with them and asked Mum to put them in water for me. It ... it was a lovely card. So was your Valentine card. I was really touched by it."

"Do you mean that?" Jon searched her eyes and it felt as if he were searching her heart also.

"Of course I do." Her heart was thumping uncomfortably as she opened her eyes as wide as they would go and gazed back at him.

He leant back in his chair and visibly relaxed. "Well, I'm glad we've got that sorted out," he said. "You can't blame me for feeling hurt, can you? It was like walking in and seeing a whole row of Valentine cards next to mine on the mantelpiece."

He thinks it's a joke, but if only he knew! Viv thought guiltily. For a moment, she suspected Jon had X-ray eyes and was scanning the contents of her dressing-table drawer. But he was neatly nibbling a prawn cracker as if nothing was wrong. The atmosphere between them was changing now, warming up, and Viv felt herself beginning to relax for the first time that day.

"You look really lovely tonight, Viv," Jon told her.

She smiled. "Thanks."

Jon sighed and stared off into the far distance somewhere. Then he brought his eyes back to hers again. "I suppose we ought to talk about the future," he said.

The whole room spun and Viv clutched the edge of the table for support. He was going to propose! Jon was going to ask her to marry him! Oh, God! How did she feel? What would she say? Her whole body began to tremble as she waited for him to say the words.

But what he said was completely unexpected. "Wonder where I'll be this time next year?"

"I…" Viv's mouth remained open as no words came. This wasn't the kind of talk about the future she had been expecting.

He went on talking as if he hadn't noticed her shocked expression. "I don't know what college I'll be going to. I could end up anywhere. This could be our last Valentine meal."

"Of course it won't be," Viv said reassuringly, giving his hand a squeeze. In return, he clutched her fingers so tightly that it hurt.

"We don't know what's going to happen," he said.

Oh, poor Jon, Viv thought. Everything's changing

for him this year. He's got the pressure of his A-levels, the awful weeks of waiting for the results, the frantic applications – just like I'll have next year.

"It'll be all right. I'll still love you," she said.

"Will you?" There was something unfamiliar in his tone, something which made her stare at him, her heart thumping uncomfortably, her hands growing icy cold. Surely he didn't doubt her? Their relationship, their love, was secure and strong. Wherever he was, she could travel to be with him. Even if he was at the opposite end of the country! She must tell him ... must convince him of her loyalty, of the extent of her love, which would make her think nothing of getting a train to the Outer Hebrides, if necessary, if they had a university there.

But she said nothing and the moment passed. The waitress appeared to clear their dishes and bring the dessert menu. Viv glanced at the clock on the restaurant wall and suddenly she was pitchforked into her parallel reality. It was a quarter past eight already. *Shane!* He was expecting her, he'd got the tickets for their night out. Oh, what was she going to do?

Guilt made her stomach clench. There was no way now that she could meet him at the White Swan as planned. But he'd told her that if, by some awful mishap, one of them was late and they missed the boat, it was making another stop at a place called Burnet's Quay at nine. So if she could get away somehow and find a taxi that could go at the speed of light... She had never needed a

miracle more. Now was the time to fake a headache, or feeling sick, or something. She actually
did feel quite ill from all the tension.

But did she want to go? Instinct told her that
Jon was at a crisis point and the thought filled
her with love for him. He needed her reassurance
that she would wait for him while he was away
studying, or that she would apply to the same
college and follow him there. She couldn't leave
him tonight. Perhaps she had better sacrifice this
boat trip, tell *Shane* the story about the headache
instead.

It would be so exciting on the boat, though.
Loads of people, great music, dancing – and he
would be waiting for her, expecting her, looking
forward to holding her in his arms as the boat
moved over the water. The words swam in front of
her eyes as she stared blankly at the menu. She
could almost feel the heat from Shane's body as he
came oh, so close to her, his lips almost touching
hers, and then that moment of panic mixed with
blissful surrender as she gave her mouth up to his
passion and – but how *could* she be thinking
about Shane like this when Jon was here, looking
so wonderful.

"I, er..." She closed the menu and looked at Jon.
"I don't think I could manage any dessert." It was
absolutely true. Her stomach was performing
somersaults and tossing around what small
amount of food she had managed to eat.

"I don't think I could, either. I'm not really very
hungry at all tonight," confessed Jon.

"Are you feeling all right?" she asked, concerned,

a fresh pang of anxiety attacking her as she spoke.

"Yes, of course I am," he answered quickly, but she noticed he was avoiding her eyes. "Er, Viv ... I don't quite know how to say this, but..."

Viv shot bolt upright in her chair. Was he about to tell her he thought they should break up? Or was this the proposal after all?

It wasn't either. "I don't know if you were expecting us to go on somewhere else after this but, well... Oh, damn it, I haven't finished my bloody essay and I've just *got* to go home and get it done because it's got to be handed in tomorrow. Will you ever forgive me?"

Rosie had been wrong, then; Fate *had* stepped in and sorted things out for her, Viv thought jubilantly. Her face split into her widest smile, but she frantically brought her lips under control and said, "Of course I will. I do understand. I really appreciate you taking me out for this meal under the circumstances. Thanks for the lovely dinner, the card, the flowers ... everything."

He asked for the bill. She leaned forward and planted a kiss on his lips. His lips held hers for a moment and she found herself responding with passion. She felt almost drunk, though she'd only had one glass of wine.

"Mmm, that was nice," Jon said. "Any more where that came from?"

They kissed again, their lips fitting together and responding in that familiar, perfect way born of trust and practice. The kisses left Viv wanting more. Everything seemed OK between them now

94

and it was the relief that was intoxicating, she realized. She felt as though she'd been walking a tightrope suspended over the Grand Canyon and had just safely reached the other side.

Jon counted out the money for the bill and Viv insisted on adding the tip. Then he helped her on with her coat and they went through the double doors of the restaurant into the freezing night air – and into another world, one in which she was setting off on a thrilling adventure which had nothing whatsoever to do with her everyday life. Shane always made her feel like that.

"You'll have more time to work if I see myself home," she said, trying not to sound impatient.

"You sure you don't mind?" He hovered with his arm around her.

"We know each other well enough now not to have to bother about polite gestures. Even on Valentine's Day," she added. "You've done enough for me today. Now go on!" She gave him a gentle shove in the direction of the bus stop.

"Thanks for being so understanding, love. What are you going to do now?" he asked.

"There's a taxi coming," she shouted, glad that she and Jon lived in opposite directions.

She waved frantically at it. " 'Bye!" she yelled as it swerved to a halt in front of her.

"I'll ring you tomorrow," Jon shouted. "Have a safe journey home!"

I hope I'll have a safe journey, too, she thought. But not home...

"Where would you like to go to, miss?" asked the taxi driver.

She wanted to reply "Into the arms of Shane Russell," but she managed to say, "Burnet's Quay, as fast as you can."

12

Will I make it? thought Viv anxiously. She peered at her watch in the gloom of the cab. Twenty to nine already! It was raining, too, great streamers of it dashing horizontally against the windows.

A quarter to ... ten to... It was a few seconds to nine as Viv paid the cabbie and sped down the quay. The boat was there, all lit up with pounding disco music coming from it. There seemed to be loads of people on board, she could see them through the windows. How would she ever find Shane? And – oh, heavens! – she didn't have a ticket. Shane had them. Her trip had been wasted. What was even worse was that the taxi had gone, she had no money, hadn't a clue where she was and the lashing rain was guaranteed to turn her hair into a frizzy mop. Why hadn't she thought to bring an umbrella with her?

Close to tears, Viv walked as far as the gangway which led on to the boat and peered at the two levels of lighted windows. It was hopeless. Even if she spotted Shane, he wouldn't hear her calling him.

"Are you coming, miss? We're going now." A member of the boat's crew, who was about to hoist up the wooden gangplank, called out to her.

"My boyfriend's on board. I was supposed to meet him at the White Swan and I was late, so I've taken a taxi here, but he's got the tickets. His name's Shane Russell. Oh please, *please* could somebody go and find him?"

The man must have realized Viv's anguish was genuine, and not an act put on by somebody trying to get into the disco for free, because he held out a hand to her and hurried her down the gangplank saying, "Come on, you can go and find him yourself."

"Oh, thank you, *thank* you!" gasped Viv gratefully. She could have kissed him, even though he was about fifty and red-faced and whiskery.

She felt the throbbing beneath her feet as the engines started up – and then they were leaving the shore and heading for the centre of the river. She spent a moment gazing through the window at the dwindling lights of Burnet's Quay, then took a deep, gulping breath. First, the Ladies to tidy up her hair and put some fresh lipstick on, and then the bar for a drink to calm her nerves. And then, to find Shane!

She had only taken a few steps when someone tapped her on the shoulder. "Viv?" a voice said uncertainly.

"Shane! Oh, how wonderful!" She hurled herself at him.

"Careful," he said with a laugh. "You'll get this all over you!" He had a glass containing some kind of orangey liquid in his hand. "Avoid the rum punch at all costs," he warned her. "It'll make your eyes fall out of your skull. What happened to you? Oh, I'm so glad you're here."

Despite her wet coat, he put his arms round her and hugged her.

"There's a cloakroom over there. You can leave your coat," he said. He hadn't taken his eyes off her for a second. The contrast between his greeting and the grumpy one she'd received from Jon couldn't have been greater.

"I ... I was late getting home, late leaving the house, the bus didn't come and it was just a disaster," she heard herself babbling.

"Well, you're here now and you can relax and enjoy yourself. Here ... let me." He helped her peel off her wet coat and then took it over to the cloakroom for her. Then he put his arm round her waist and steered her in the direction of the room where the food and drink were.

"White wine, please," Viv requested, desperately smoothing her hair with her hands.

Shane placed his unfinished glass on a table and asked for a Coke instead. "I want to be fit to drive you home tonight," he explained.

They got their drinks and walked hand in hand along the oak-panelled corridor to the room where the disco was.

"You look really lovely," Shane said. "That's the

dress you were wearing the night we met, isn't it?"

"Yes. Sorry I haven't got a very extensive wardrobe."

"If you've got something which really suits you, then it doesn't matter how often you wear it," he reassured her. "It's funny, red doesn't suit a lot of people but it looks great on you, with that stunning black hair of yours."

"Thanks," Viv said shyly, thinking how delectable he was looking in reddish-black 501s and a red and black check lumberjack shirt open over a black T-shirt. Very colour-coordinated! Not for the first time, she wondered if he didn't have some lurking talent as an artist as well as his writing and music skills.

Viv halted outside the door to the big room where everyone was dancing. "I'm not too dressed up, am I?" she asked anxiously.

"No way. There's people wearing all sorts of things from shorts to floor-length dresses. Come on, let's put these drinks down and dance."

The floor was packed but Shane found a space and hauled her laughing into it. They danced three long, fast ones in succession.

"Whew!" said Viv, panting. "Let's have a rest."

But just then the tempo changed to a slow number. "No, just dance this one with me, please," Shane begged. "I've been dreaming of doing this all night."

Someone dimmed the lights. Girls squealed and then fell silent as they were pulled into their partners' arms. Shane put his arms round Viv and she moved in close to him, so that their bodies were pressed together as one unit while their feet found a mutual rhythm, a slow sort of shuffle, barely moving, just swaying from side to side.

Shane's hand moved up Viv's back and buried itself in her hair. He bent her head towards his so that their lips hovered for a second within touching distance, so close that she could feel his breath against her skin.

"Oh, Viv..." he whispered and then the gap closed and his warm lips brushed hers, releasing such a flood of feelings within her that she felt herself trembling against him. A golden light was beating against her closed eyelids. It was as if her heart had been turned on like a lantern and was illuminating her from the inside. She had never felt like this before. His lips moved against hers, sometimes fragile and delicate as tissue paper, other times pressing and straining as if trying to taste the very essence of her soul.

Every bit of her seemed to touch every bit of him, from feet to forehead. She was dizzy, she was lost, she was ... in love? Could she be? What was it he was murmuring, his lips pressed against the corner of her mouth, his nose gently nudging hers in an Eskimo kiss?

"I love you, Viv."

Did he say it? Or had she misheard?

"Can you say that again?" she whispered. "The music ... I didn't quite catch—"

"I told you I loved you. But then you must have guessed."

His eyelashes, long and dark for one so fair,

brushed against her cheek as he opened his eyes and pulled his head slightly back, focusing. Their eyes met and held, his midnight blue ones and her hazel ones. Viv was so spellbound, she couldn't even blink. She had been struck dumb, too. She couldn't say a word, she could only nod, her lips slightly apart as she poured her heart's feelings through her eyes into his.

"The first time I saw you, it was love at first sight," he told her, "but I couldn't say anything until now. I was scared of frightening you off. I had to be sure how you felt."

I haven't said how I feel, Viv thought. What has he read in my eyes? Does he really mean it, or does he say this to every girl? No, she couldn't believe that. What was pouring from his eyes was too intense to be an act. Yes, she believed he really did love her.

"I got your card. Music is the food of love, all right, and vice versa. Love's the food of music! You've really inspired me to write," he said. "I've never written so many songs and poems before."

"I got yours, too – and the flowers. They were beautiful. Did you paint the card?" She could at least talk again, but she still felt as if she were in a trance. Her voice seemed to be coming from a long way away.

"It was my idea and I asked Jane to paint it for me."

"It was heaps better than any shop one. I'll keep it for ever."

"Will you?"

Some instinct told Viv that Shane was talking

about more than the card. "Yes, of course I will," she answered softly.

The music changed but the tempo was still slow and dreamy. Suddenly, Viv recognized the song. "Oh, no, it's *Lady In Red*," she said, laughing.

"I know. I asked Steve to play it," Shane admitted.

She squeezed her arms tightly round him. "What would you have done if I'd been wearing green?"

"I'd have had to write a new hit song," he said. "Or else record an updated version of *Greensleeves*."

Viv laughed and closed her eyes and they swayed in an embrace, pressed tightly together, their feet barely moving, his chin resting on her hair. He'd said he loved her. It was in the open now. He hadn't asked her if she loved him, but she knew he would be wondering, and sooner or later he *would* ask her.

And I do, she thought dreamily, raising her face as he placed a gentle kiss on her forehead then sprinkled her face with them, like rain. *I do love him. Tonight, on this boat, in his arms, listening to this music, I love him*. Tomorrow? What was that? It didn't exist.

At twelve-thirty, the boat gently bumped back against Burnet's Quay. At one, it arrived back at the landing stage of the riverside pub, the White Swan. Shane drove her home and asked if he could see her the next night and she had to say no because she had a pile of schoolwork to do.

"Well, I've got a solid four nights of rehearsals

and gigs with *Bombshell* after that," he said, looking rather forlorn.

"That means we won't see each other for nearly a week!" she protested.

"I'll see what I can do. I'll give you a ring," he promised.

They clung together for a long kiss and then, reluctantly, Viv slid out of the van, wincing as her tired, painful feet met the hard pavement.

"Thanks for a fantastic time," she said, blowing him a kiss.

"Good night, darling," Shane said.

The van rumbled off and Viv pushed open the front gate and slowly and silently ascended the staircase, Shane's "darling" echoing in her ears like the final perfect chord in a beautiful piece of music. "Good night, darling..." Jon had said that to her often enough, but it didn't have the effect of making her feel so warm and melty inside.

She reached out to open her bedroom door and her eyes were drawn to a note that was stuck there. It was in her father's handwriting and it said, *Jon rang 10.30pm.*

13

Jon rang again before she left for school in the morning. Although Viv had racked her brains to think up an alibi, before tumbling into a deep and dreamless sleep, her imagination had, for once, failed her.

"I rang to see if you'd got home all right and to apologize for ruining the evening, and when your dad said you weren't there and he'd thought you were with me, I was worried sick. I had images of the taxi crashing, or you being abducted on the way home ... all kinds of things."

"I'm sorry." Viv was hanging her head and biting her lip even though he couldn't see her.

"I even rang Trish to see if you were there. Where on earth did you get to?"

Thank heavens he'd said that, Viv thought; that was the very excuse she'd been about to make!

"You were almost right. I dropped in at Rosie's, but she was out with Nita, so I came home after that." She would have to prime Rosie and hope she'd agree to stand alibi for her.

Fortunately, Jon decided not to do any further probing. "I was ringing to say I'd like to make it up to you for having dashed off so unromantically last night," he said. "How about a film on Friday? What's that one you said you wanted to see?"

They made arrangements to meet and once their phone conversation was over, Viv found herself feeling heaps happier. Things felt as if they were back to normal now and thank heavens they were. She needed Jon's constancy, his reliability. Knowing he loved her and was always there provided a kind of springboard for everything else she did in her life ... even her illicit dates with Shane. On her own, without the security of a loving boyfriend, would she have been able to cope with Shane's unpredictable lifestyle, the way he was always disappearing with the band for long hours of rehearsals, and last-minute gigs? She'd never be able to make any plans for them to do things, he'd always be messing up her arrangements, something Jon never did.

But isn't that what you like about him, too? insisted that voice in her head that certainly wasn't the voice of her conscience! It was his very unpredictability that helped to make him so exciting. There was something about Shane, some hidden inner core, that she couldn't fathom, and it was this core that gave rise to his creativity, his vital spark, even his romantic feelings about her...

She went off to school that morning with Shane very much on her mind. Maybe it was a presentiment of what was to come.

"Viv?" Trish approached Viv at break with a very serious look on her face. "Look, you're not going to like this, but I've got to tell you. It's about Shane."

"Don't tell me something's happened to him! What is it?" Viv felt fear weakening her limbs.

"No, nothing's happened. At least, not to him. It's…" Trish stopped and bit her lip, shoving her hands deep into the pockets of her black raincoat.

Viv felt like shaking her, she was so impatient to hear whatever it was. "Go on, tell me," she urged through gritted teeth.

"You know Sandra Bennett, that prefect who left last year? You know, the one everyone said was pregnant?"

"Yes, I remember. The one whose sister works in Miss Selfridge. She gave me a sneaky discount once when I—"

"Shut up and listen." Trish placed a restraining hand on Viv's arm. Viv didn't want to shut up and listen. She felt she didn't want to hear what Trish was about to say. But Trish seemed determined that Viv should hear the truth, if truth it was…

"I'm telling you this for your own good, so that you know what you're getting involved with. People say that she was Shane's girlfriend for a while. She met him at one of those pub gigs he plays. He got her pregnant and refused to have anything to do with her. That's what they say."

Viv felt a jolt of white-hot shock. Then anger rose up her spine and into her throat. "Who are 'they'?" she snapped.

"I mustn't, it wouldn't be fair," Trish replied.

"Just trust me. And if you have any doubts, ask Sandra's sister. You know where she is."

"I can't do that!" Viv wailed. The bell was ringing to signal the end of break, but she didn't want to go. How was she expected to concentrate on French with this nasty piece of gossip rankling in her brain?

"Well, I'm just passing on the information for your own good. I don't want to see you getting hurt – or, even worse, ending up like Sandra," Trish said. "You haven't exactly known him very long, have you? There might be all sorts of things about him that you don't know. He could be on drugs, or anything!"

"No, he isn't!" Viv tore herself away from Trish and went into her classroom, in a state of wild anger and turbulence. As she was setting her books out on the desk in front of her, she began to calm down and think about what Trish had said.

Shane didn't seem the type to abandon a pregnant girlfriend. You'd have to be a very hard person to do that; he was too soft and emotional. She could imagine that if Shane ever became a father, he would dote on the baby.

She had a sudden image of him rocking a small baby in his arms, with such a look of love flooding from his eyes and curving around his mouth that she found her eyes welling with tears. *That* was the sort of person he was, she felt sure. Even if, for various reasons, he didn't get on with the mother, he would never abandon the child, but would want to be part of its upbringing.

On the other hand, Trish was right about her

not having known Shane long. A month *wasn't* very long – but ever since she first caught sight of him, she felt as if she had known him all her life. And longer. She seemed to have known him for ever, in other lives, too, if reincarnation existed. There had been such a sense of recognition when their eyes first met, as if their very souls were greeting each other as long-lost lovers.

What if it was all a trick, though? What if those candid blue eyes masked a demonic ability to lull girls into a sense of false security, make them fall in love with him? Perhaps all she was was another notch on his scorecard. Yet instinct told her that this wasn't true ... that he was being sincere when he said he loved her. How could he have written that song for her if the emotions behind it hadn't been true ones? Or was he such a skilful songwriter that he could produce them at the drop of a hat?

There was only one way to find out, and that was to try and remain completely objective next time she saw him. She would try to dam up her feelings and be critical, assess him as if he were a stranger to her. She would quiz him about ex-girlfriends and drop the name of Sandra Bennett casually into the conversation, to see what his reaction was. And then...

Viv had arranged to meet Jon outside the cinema at seven, as the film started at seven-thirty. Just as she was going out of the front door, the phone rang and she heard her mother calling out, "Viv? Are you still here? It's for you!"

She stopped dead in her tracks. It could be Trish, or Rosie, but what if it were Shane and her mother said she'd gone to the movies with her boyfriend!

She dashed back but it was too late, her mother had replaced the receiver.

"Who was it?" she questioned breathlessly.

"I thought it was Jonathan at first and I nearly said, 'Hello, Jonathan,' but you were lucky I didn't because it was that other boy who keeps ringing you up. Shane."

Viv tried to sound disinterested, ignoring the questions in her mother's eyes. "Oh? What did he say?"

"He asked where you were and I said you'd gone to the Odeon with a *friend*." Mrs McCulloch stressed the word firmly, giving Viv a look as much as to say, *There, aren't I good to you?*

"Thanks, Mum," Viv said dutifully. "But what did he say?"

"Nothing much, just that he'd ring another time. I hope you know what you're doing, Viv..."

"Sorry, Mum, I must dash, I'll be late for Jon." Viv flew out of the house and away from what might have turned into a major interrogation.

A bus came straight away and she was only five minutes late.

"Hi, sweetheart, I've already bought the tickets," Jon announced brightly. As he placed his arm around her waist and ushered her into the cinema, Viv had a quick, stealthy look round. Her mother had mentioned that she had gone to the Odeon, so there was an outside chance that Shane might come here, to find her and talk to her.

There was no sign of him or his van. She was safe to relax in Jon's company and enjoy the film. She couldn't stand it when her two worlds almost collided like this. It played havoc with her nerves and made her feel sick and uneasy. *Dangerous Game* ... that was the title of one of *Bombshell*'s heavier songs. And that was precisely what she was playing, though it didn't seem like a game at all. It was much too serious for that.

They had twenty minutes before the film started so they had a coffee each at the café-bar to warm them up and then found aisle seats near the back. Jon put his arm around her shoulders and she snuggled against him, then both were soon absorbed in the film, too immersed even to kiss.

Afterwards, he asked if she was hungry, but she wasn't.

"I was going to suggest fish and chips," he said.

"How about tomorrow?" They usually went out somewhere on Saturday night.

"Oh, tomorrow..." Jon gave a grimace. "Sorry, Viv, I'm a bit tied up tomorrow. I told Tony I'd go and watch his football match in the afternoon and after that it's drinks with the lads, I'm afraid. You don't mind *too* much, do you? We could do something on Sunday instead."

"Yes, I suppose so," Viv said, feeling suddenly deflated. They *always* went out on Saturday night – for two whole years they'd hardly missed one. And now he was putting football before her! Were they getting into a rut? Was he going off her?

"Thanks for being so understanding, love. I'll walk you to the bus stop," Jon said. He seemed in a really good mood, which just served to make Viv feel even more despondent. She hadn't realized before how much she relied on Jon, how much his very predictability meant to her. When he changed their routine like this, she felt suddenly insecure.

Which perhaps was why, when he took her in his arms to kiss her goodbye when her bus was in sight, she responded with such keen passion that he gave her a head-whirling kiss back which took half the journey home to recover from.

And kept her awake for hours that night. If Jon's kisses could still have such a mind-blowing effect on her, where did that leave her with Shane? she agonized. It would be far easier if she felt she was going off Jon. But she wasn't. And if he seemed to be going off her, she knew she'd be devastated.

But if *Shane* said he didn't want to see her any more, she'd be dreadfully upset. It would be like somebody cancelling Christmas, or saying birthdays were no longer to be celebrated.

Shane is my special treat, she reasoned. He's like a big, delicious, forbidden box of chocolates that I can't stop eating. Nobody's going to take him away from me and I can't give him up.

14

She rang Shane at lunchtime on Saturday but got no reply. She tried again at six, and again at seven but although she let it ring for ages in case he was in the bathroom, or in Jane's flat, in the end she had to admit defeat.

Rosie and Trish were also out, Jon was at his booze-up ... it seemed everyone in the world was enjoying themselves except her. And it was so long since she'd seen Shane. He'd said he'd be busy for four days. Well, the four days would be up on Monday and she couldn't wait. Not only did she desperately want to see him, but she had the Sandra mystery to clear up, too. Though, as far as she was concerned, the verdict was absolutely Not Guilty!

Next morning, Jon arrived unexpectedly early with the great suggestion that they take a train down to London as his aunt, who was a member of a society which supported London Zoo, had given him two free tickets.

Viv had only ever been to London twice, so she

was really excited. Her father gave them a lift to the station and by lunchtime they were through the entrance gate and standing by the Aquarium.

"I can't be bothered with fish, I'd rather see the lions and tigers," Viv said, feeling like a kid again as she tugged Jon's hand.

"Oh, let's just have a quick dash round," Jon said. "We'll visit your tigers next, and then it's my turn again. I fancy either the tarantulas or the bats."

"Oh, yuk!" said Viv disgustedly.

The Aquarium was a magical experience. In one tank a wonderful creature called a Lipstick Tang, with big red filmstar lips, was nibbling a chunk of greenery in such a comical way that Viv couldn't help laughing. A few metres away she was nose to nose with a turtle through the thick glass. And as for the sharks! Although only small, their malevolent beady eyes and mouths like gashes in their heads made Viv shudder. Their skin was so smooth, their bodies so streamlined that they looked like the first class aquatic weapons that they were.

"I can see where so many car stylists got their inspiration from," Jon said, studying them intently.

Viv was glad to reach the newts and frogs by the exit. They had an argument about whether the extremely still, shiny frog they spotted behind some leaves was plastic or real, then it suddenly gave a huge leap towards them, making Viv jump backwards, and clung to the front of the glass for a few seconds with its toes spread out.

114

. "I'll look twice at your mum's garden gnomes now," Viv commented.

The yawning lions were sprawled lazily in their enclosure and a tiger, prone on a concrete slab, moved nothing but its stripy brow, which rippled as a fly landed on it.

"Well, the kings of the jungle were a bit boring. Let's see if the bats are awake," said Jon, making for the Moonlight World in the Small Mammal House.

They certainly were. One in particular looked so like a friend of Jon's who had a rather unfortunate squashed-looking face and sticky-out ears that they instantly named it Barry Bat.

They had a wonderful day. At twenty to four, as they were leaving, Viv suddenly realized, with a lurch of both her heart and her conscience, that she hadn't thought about Shane for hours, she'd been so absorbed in looking at the animals and chattering away to Jon.

It's probably a good thing, she told herself. Nobody can suffer all day, every day. Today is for me and Jon.

They made a detour through Camden Market on their way back to the Tube station and as they poked around various stalls, remarking on some of the more outrageous fashions and weird and wonderful things on sale, Viv felt as if time had rolled back. This was the kind of fun day out they had had a year ago ... two years ago. Before Jon had started swotting seriously for his A-levels. Before their relationship had calmed down, or grown up, or whatever it had done.

She gave Jon's hand a squeeze and he responded by putting his arm around her waist and pulling her close to him.

"I've really enjoyed today," he murmured, nuzzling her hair as they paused by a stall selling New Age crystals and jewellery.

"So have I – it's been fantastic!" she enthused.

"We're good friends, us two, aren't we?" he said.

She wrinkled her brow. "Just friends?" she remarked. "I thought we were a bit more than that..."

"Of course we are! I didn't mean that. What I meant was, we get on really well as well as going out together. You'd be surprised how many people don't. Some people can be madly in love yet just can't get on most of the time. They argue like crazy, yet they're still nuts about each other. Funny, isn't it?"

"Who do you know who's like that?" Viv asked. She couldn't think of any mutual friends of theirs who behaved that way.

"Oh, you don't know them," he said vaguely and at that moment Viv's eye was caught by a fabulous silk cushion which would look perfect in her bedroom. It turned out to be far too expensive.

"Come on, we'd better be heading back," Jon said. It was dark and the stallholders were beginning to close their stalls.

They had a burger and a Coke apiece from the buffet on the Birmingham train, then had to wait three quarters of an hour for the connection to their local station.

"It feels as if we've been away for weeks," said

Viv when they arrived back at Marshdale at ten to eleven. "Today was like a holiday."

"Yes," agreed Jon. "I don't know when I'll be able to take another whole day out from work. Do you realize I'll be sitting my exams in three months? I'm feeling quite panicky about it. If I'm a bit elusive over the next few weeks, Viv, I hope you understand. It's going to be work, work, work. I'll be either in the library or shut up at home."

"You make it sound really gloomy," Viv said, her happy mood starting to evaporate.

"In the short term, it will be. I'm just telling you now so that you're forewarned. I don't want you thinking that I'm deliberately neglecting you."

"We're going to miss our last buses if we continue this conversation much longer," Viv pointed out agitatedly. She had already seen a 36 pulling in to the stand. They were at the terminus so it would probably leave in a few minutes.

"Yes, but it's a conversation we need to have," Jon said.

Viv looked at him and suddenly felt as if she were seeing him for the first time. Who was this tall, dark, thin boy with the solemn brown eyes? Did she know him? He was very attractive, but, if she had never seen him before, she would have thought how serious and withdrawn and studious he appeared.

There were dark shadows beneath his eyes and a sort of pinched look around his mouth. He'd said he was a bit tired and had a slight hangover from the previous night, but it looked more like overwork to her.

"I'm worried about you working too hard," she said, searching his face anxiously.

He smiled, and at once turned back into the old warm, affectionate, familiar, sparkly Jon. She heaved a sharp sigh of relief. Maybe *she* was feeling tired, too.

"Don't worry, we've had a couple of lessons on Study Skills and I think I know how to pace myself and when to take breaks from it," he assured her.

"OK. Give us a kiss, my bus is about to go," she said hastily, offering him her lips.

His mouth met hers and their lips clung briefly, leaving her wanting more.

"I'll ring you soon," he said. "I'll see you before the end of the week."

"I hope so," she said, placing one foot on the platform of the bus.

"Viv?"

Jon's voice froze her in her tracks. She turned her head round.

"Come on, we haven't got all night," urged the bus conductor.

"What is it?" she asked Jon anxiously.

He appeared to change his mind. "Oh, nothing. It can wait," he said.

She boarded the bus and puzzled about it all the way home.

Next morning she managed to put it out of her mind when Rosie told her coyly that she'd been to a party on Saturday and had got off with a boy called Wilson.

"Is that his first name or his surname?" asked Viv, as they sat in the canteen eating sandwiches.

"I don't know," said Rosie.

"Maybe he's called Wilson Wilson – you never know. After all, there's that shop called Owen Owen!"

"Well, he's gorgeous, anyway. I'm seeing him on Wednesday. What did you do over the weekend?"

"You've got pickle on the end of your nose. I went to see a film with Jon on Friday – it was a Hugh Grant one, better not tell Trish – and then Jon and I went to the Zoo in London yesterday. We went to Camden Lock afterwards. I've never seen so many freaky looking people. There was one man in a—"

"Trish said she went to a Hugh Grant film on Saturday," Rosie butted in.

"Oh? Who with?" Viv asked interestedly. If Trish had a new boyfriend, then she felt she had a right to know about it.

"Haven't a clue. You know what Trish is like. If she doesn't want to tell you something, she won't. You could suspend her over Niagara Falls upside down on the end of a bungee and she still wouldn't say a word." Rosie blotted the end of her nose at last with a paper tissue.

"You know, I think Trish would make a wonderful spy," Viv pointed out. "Even if they tortured her she'd never betray her country. Where is she, by the way?"

"Had to go to the dentist's, talking of torture. Want a piece of Kit-Kat?"

Viv nodded, so Rosie snapped off a piece and

handed it to her with the end wrapped in a corner of tinfoil from the wrapper.

"Ta. I thought I hadn't seen her. What's she up to, I wonder? I mean, I've told her all *my* deadly secrets," said Viv, demolishing half the chocolate biscuit in one bite. "Come to think of it, I haven't seen much of her lately."

"That's probably more your fault than hers, with two boyfriends on the go," Rosie pointed out. "Though I haven't seen that much of her out of school, either. You know how she always used to ring us every night for a gossip? Well, I'm lucky if I hear from her once a week now."

"Perhaps her mum's had a moan about the phone bill," Viv suggested.

"Could be. But ... oh, I don't know. I can't quite put my finger on it, Viv, but she's been a bit odd lately. You probably haven't noticed, with so much going on in your life, but—"

"I *have* noticed," Viv said. "But I thought it was because she didn't approve of my seeing Shane and she was avoiding me. So ... who *did* she go to the cinema with?"

Rosie shrugged. "It was probably her sister, but she'd rather have us think it was with a boy."

Viv decided Rosie was right.

She felt light-hearted all afternoon, half expecting Shane to be outside school in his white van. The fact that there was no sign of him didn't dent her high spirits as she felt sure that he'd ring that evening. But he didn't. Neither did Jon, but she didn't expect a call from him. He was busy working, after all. She rang Trish, but she was out.

Tuesday came and went. Trish said she and her sister had gone to visit an aunt, an explanation which satisfied both Viv and Rosie.

There was no white van to meet her that afternoon and no phone call from Shane that evening, though Jon rang to ask her to meet him after school on Thursday. He sounded a bit distracted. He *is* overworking, thought Viv worriedly.

But her anxiety about Shane's whereabouts vastly surpassed any anxiety she felt about Jon's state of mental health.

"I can't stand it!" she told her pillow, through gritted teeth. "I just can't stand it!" she repeated, shaking the pillow as though shaking the bars of a cage she was trapped in. In a way, she was – a cage of ignorance, of not knowing what was going on.

What's happened to him? she fretted. Has he met someone else? Is it true about Sandra? Has she had the baby and they've gone off and got married? Have his band suddenly been sent on a tour of Outer Mongolia? Why doesn't he just *tell* me! Anything would be better than this silence in which her imagination was free to produce all kinds of nightmare situations.

On Wednesday, she was put out of her misery at last. Shane rang at ten to seven, sounding very croaky indeed and saying that all *Bombshell*'s gigs had had to be cancelled because both he and Den, the drummer, had got flu.

"I don't know if you tried ringing me – I heard the phone go a few times – but I couldn't get out of bed to answer it because every time I stood up I felt dizzy and my head ached like hell," he said.

121

"And I couldn't call you because I'd lost my voice!"

"Oh, you poor thing, I wish you'd told me!" Viv's sense of relief was so terrific that she was aware of sounding ecstatic, rather than sympathetic. "I could have come round with medicine and grapes and things if I'd known."

"What? And risk catching it yourself? I wasn't having that!" Shane said. "I knew you'd want to come round and play Florence Nightingale, that's why I didn't tell you."

"Well, can I come round now?" she asked, crossing her fingers and praying that he'd say yes.

She imagined him lying in bed, his face pale and drawn, his hair like tousled straw on the pillow, his body racked with coughs. She would make him soup and sit there spoon-feeding him, watching the colour come back to his cheeks. She would place ice on his brow to cool his fever and read poetry to him until he fell asleep, whereupon she would tiptoe out and switch out the light, having first scribbled three little words on a piece of paper and left it by his bedside: *Get well soon.* Or dare she write those other three little words, the ones she'd only ever said to Jon...?

"I'd rather you didn't," he said in answer to her question. "I don't want anyone to see me with my nose as red as this, especially not you. Wait till Friday. I'll see you then. We've got a gig at the Eagle. We'll have a drink there to celebrate my recovery. I've missed you, you know."

"I've missed you, too," breathed Viv, adding to herself, *you don't know how much!*

15

On Thursday evening when Viv walked into The Pier, the recently opened wine bar by the river where she'd arranged to meet Jon, she found him sitting on a stool at the bar.

He swung round to greet her. "I saw you in the mirror behind the bar," he explained. He had the widest, most enthusiastic grin on his face that she'd seen for a long time. What's got into him? Viv wondered.

"I bought you these," he said, thrusting a bunch of flowers at her.

"For *me*?" she said disbelievingly. Jon wasn't the flowers type, apart from on special occasions like birthdays and Valentine's Day. She parted the florist's paper wrap and the glorious scent of freesias wafted up to her nostrils.

"Mmm! They're gorgeous. Thanks ever so, though I don't know what I've done to deserve them!"

"Just being you, that's all." He was still smiling that smile.

She gave him a kiss on the cheek. "It's nice in here, isn't it?" she commented, looking round. The floorboards had been painted sea green. All the furniture was bamboo and wicker, though the round bamboo tables had glass tops. Everything was in Mediterranean greens and blues and posters of Greek islands and tropical shores decorated the walls.

"Haven't you been here before?" Jon sounded surprised.

"No. Why, have you?" she asked him.

"Yes, I came in one day last week, with some people from college. I could have sworn I'd been in here with you, too. I'm probably mixing it up with that pasta place we've been to, that's got all this wicker stuff as well. You know the one I mean."

It crossed her mind that perhaps he'd been in here with another girl. But who? He didn't have time to date anyone else. He barely had time for her at the moment. Unless it was someone from his sixth form college class and they sat and discussed chemistry theorems over glasses of wine.

No, she thought. She was being over-suspicious. If Jon was really being unfaithful to her, he'd be more careful. His explanation sounded believable enough. She was only being suspicious because of her own situation. Besides, he was so loyal and straight and trustworthy, he just wasn't the unfaithful type. Not like me, she told herself ashamedly...

Jon insisted on buying her a marvellous fruity cocktail which cost the earth. "I've missed you,

Fluffy-head. Sunday was great, wasn't it?" he said.

"Mm, it was," she agreed.

"Are you OK sitting here? Not too near the door and the draughts?" he enquired.

"Yes, I'm fine, thanks."

"Things going well at school? Did you get that German translation done all right?"

"Just about. I got a B, so I suppose that's not too bad..."

He was paying her so much attention that it was almost as if they were on one of their very first dates. He's feeling guilty, that's what it is, she thought. But not about any infidelity. He's trying to make up for putting his work before me, that's why he's being so nice. And I'm doing the same thing, she realized suddenly. Her own guilt about Shane was making her extra attentive to Jon – extra demonstrative, too. She wanted to give him big kisses and cuddles, to assure him that she still loved him. It was almost as if, the keener she got on Shane, the more passionate she was towards Jon.

Jon started stroking her hand. "You've got such lovely smooth skin. It doesn't get all chapped in the cold weather like mine does," he said.

"That's because boys don't use hand cream and moisturizer," she said.

"We don't want to go round smelling like a perfume shop," he said. "Well, most of us don't..."

"There are some which are just for men, with a more masculine scent in them," Viv pointed out.

"Talking about scent, what's that one you usually wear?" Jon asked.

"You mean Dewberry?"

He said nothing, just delved into his pocket and handed her a small package. When she opened it, a tiny blue bottle of Dewberry essential oil nestled inside.

"Oh, wow, Jon! This is the really strong one which lasts for ages because you can mix it with stuff which dilutes it," she said, thrilled. "It's marvellous. I'd nearly run out as well. It's not my birthday, though..." she added, fixing him with a long, searching look.

"I know it's not," Jon said. He flashed her a smile and turned her hand over and started gently stroking her palm with his index finger. He'd never done that before. What *has* got into him? she thought.

"Well," she said, "if this is your way of showing me you love me, I shan't knock it."

"I do love you and I don't want you to forget it," he said. There was something especially meaningful in his tone of voice. Viv stared at him. Something wasn't quite right... Something was definitely up.

A very unpleasant feeling washed over her, leaving her feeling sick and shaky. He knows, she thought; he knows! This is his way of trying to win me back, by being extra nice to me and spending money on me. Some rotten person has dropped me in it!

"I thought we might have a bite to eat here," he was saying, though she could hardly hear him through the panic that was throbbing in her ears. "I'm starving!"

"Er ... could we wait just a little bit?" she said weakly. "I ... I'm not quite ready to eat yet."

Jon was broke, she knew that; he couldn't afford to splash out on expensive wine bar food. But he seemed determined.

"Let's have a look at the menu, anyway. Mmm ... *Croque Monsieur*. Just a fancy name for a toasted sandwich. I think I quite fancy a ham and cheese one. They do chicken, too, Fluffy. You like chicken, don't you?"

"Yes," she answered absently.

The next minute, he was ordering, yet she knew she wouldn't be able to eat a thing! He was gazing so intently at her, too. Then she felt his foot come sneaking under the table and wiggle its way between hers. It sat there, with her feet on either side of it. Normally, it would have felt snug and exciting, a secret little gesture of love. Now, it felt intrusive to have his foot there. She wanted to take hers away, tuck them far under her chair where he couldn't reach them.

"What's up?" he asked her. "You're in a funny mood tonight."

"I could say the same about you," she retorted.

"Oh, come on! Here I am doing my best to spoil you a bit because I haven't seen you for so long, and you don't appreciate it," he grumbled.

"Of course I do!" Her face relaxed into a tender smile. So he hadn't found out about her and Shane. Her instinct that he was trying to compensate for his workload was right.

Suddenly, her appetite came roaring audibly back. "Oops!" she said, patting her tummy. "It seems I *am* hungry after all." And she started tucking into her toasted sandwich.

The wine bar was quite packed by now, mainly with workers from nearby shops and offices. They were lucky that they had come in when they did.

After finishing the last crumb, they ordered coffee and sat back in their chairs. Jon took her hand again and held it captured in his. He still had that intent, searching look in his eyes. She began to feel a teeny bit uneasy again.

"I'm going to take you home tonight, right to the door," he insisted. "It's ages since I've said hello to your mum and dad."

"They'll be pleased to see you," she said. "That's if they're in. It's Mum's yoga night and Dad might be over at Uncle Brian's."

"I rather hope they're *not* in!" he said.

There was an extra sparkle in his eyes which Viv knew only too well. In the past, she would have welcomed the opportunity for a lengthy kissing session in the lounge, but now... Well, a brief kiss or two was OK, but any more and she knew she would be thinking guiltily about Shane, especially as she was seeing him the very next night.

And tomorrow night, she thought, when I'm kissing Shane I'll be curled up with guilt about Jon. I can't win! Her heart felt heavy as lead. Oh Jon, she thought, glancing at his fabulous profile, why do you have to be so gorgeous and adorable? Why am I taking such a risk of hurting you when I love you so much?

They got home and her dad was in, watching

telly. Viv had seldom felt so pleased to see him. Saved! she thought. Jon drank a cup of coffee, then said he had to go.

Viv went to the door with him and opened it. Jon lingered on the step. He pulled Viv into his arms and forced a passionate kiss on her, tongue in the mouth and everything!

"No," she said agitatedly. "Not here. Everyone can see!" She actually felt as if she was being watched, and glanced at all the curtains opposite to see if any were twitching.

"Sorry," he said. "I've been dying to kiss you properly for ages. I'll be a good boy and go now. 'Bye, love, I'll ring you tomorrow or the day after."

"Not tomorrow," she said hastily, "I'm going out to hear a band. With Rosie," she added quickly.

"Have a good time," he said and blew her a kiss as he walked off.

She waved enthusiastically, then closed the door and leaned against it, feeling completely over-whelmed. A Jon who was preoccupied with work, and was distant and casual, was one thing, but this passionate, demonstrative new Jon was too much for her to cope with any more. Though she loathed to have to think about it, all her instincts screamed that it was time to make a decision. She didn't know if she had the courage to do it. One of them, either Jon or Shane, would have to go – and what a heartbreaking choice it was going to be...

16

Shane's gig was cancelled. He met her after school and told her so. "Jump in," he said. "I've bought some food and I'm going to cook you a meal tonight."

"You mean you can cook as well? Is there no end to this boy's talents?" joked Viv as she swung herself up into the passenger seat of the van.

"You're not allergic to anything, I hope?"

"Not really. There's a few things I don't like. Tripe – ugh, I can't stand even looking at it! – mussels because they made me ill once, and I'm a bit funny with strawberries. But that's it…"

She was aware that Shane's face had fallen. "Oh, no!" he said. "That's ruined everything. I'd found this amazing French recipe for tripe in mussel sauce and I'd planned strawberry mousse for dessert."

She gasped, "Oh, dear. I…" Then her voice tailed off when his mouth twitched and she realized he'd been joking.

"It's cold in here," she said, rubbing her hands.

"Sorry, the heater's packed up on me. I'll have to take it in. Give me a hand."

Viv held out her right hand. Very delicately, he drew it to his lips, his eyes on the road all the while, and sucked each finger in turn into his mouth and held it there until he'd warmed up the icy digit. Then he turned over the palm of her hand and kissed it and returned it to her, saying, "Now the other one."

There must be something about my hands, thought Viv, recalling how tenderly Jon had stroked her hand the night before. She shivered with pleasure as he played his tongue up and down her finger. There was something about this treatment which was even more intimate than a kiss.

"Better?" he asked.

"Yes, much."

"I'd better not try and warm anything else up or I'll crash the van!" he said.

He started to sing. Viv loved listening to him. There was something so free and happy-go-lucky about Shane. He didn't seem to have any inhibitions about anything. She felt that whatever he wanted to say, he'd come right out and say it, and whatever he wanted to, he'd do. Unlike Jon, who seemed far more uptight and hesitant about everything.

Maybe this was the time to ask him about the main thing on her mind; was there any truth in the rumour about him and Sandra? She *had* to know. She waited till he got to the end of the song he was singing, then steeled herself. "Shane?" she asked.

"That's me!" he answered jokily.

"Shane, did you ever go out with a girl called Sandra Bennett?"

He put on a thoughtful expression. "Now, let me see... There was Anneka Rice – she was the first. Then there was Sharon Stone, Naomi Campbell and Cindy Crawford – oh, and Catherine Zeta Jones was in between. But nobody called Sandra Bennett, I'm afraid."

"Shane, I'm serious!" Viv complained.

He took his eyes off the road for a second and give her a swift but straight-faced glance. "So am I. I've never met a Sandra Bennett. Never heard of her. Why?"

"Oh ... nothing, really. Just something my friend Trish said. She knows Sandra's sister."

"Well, if this Sandra's nice, better introduce her then. *And* her sister!" joked the incorrigible Shane.

"You're horrible!" Viv protested, grinning in spite of herself. Somehow, this inane bit of conversation had convinced her Shane was speaking the truth and a weight was off her mind.

Shane started talking about his mother in Macclesfield, and his two sisters. Viv listened with interest. His sisters were called Sharon and Charlotte – or Charlie, as they all called her.

"Sharon, Charlotte and Shane ... all your names begin with a *sh*," Viv pointed out.

"Just Mum's whim at the time. They say pregnant women get funny ideas."

132

There's that word again, thought Viv. He wouldn't be able to throw it into a conversation so easily if he had a guilty conscience. No, he was definitely Not Guilty.

"There aren't many names beginning with sh. What if she'd called you Sharif, like Omar Sharif?" Viv said.

"Or, even worse, Shep, like in the Elvis Presley song about the old dog!"

He began to sing it and they both giggled. By this time they were just turning into Shane's road. When Viv walked into his flat, she discovered that he'd dragged the heavy kitchen table into the living room and had draped it in heavy crimson velvet in place of a tablecloth. Three red candles were in a triple candlestick in the centre of the table. Shane lit them. Then he poured them both a glass of red wine.

"Do you need any help in the kitchen?" she enquired, taking one of the two seats at the table.

"No. You just sit right there and wait. I'll only be a moment."

"Oh!" Viv gasped in amazement when she looked at the two dishes Shane brought in. He had sliced an avocado and arranged the pale green segments in a circle round both plates, interspersed with slices of pale mozzarella cheese, scarlet tomato and very thin slices of orange. The result was so artistic and colourful that it was worthy of being painted by Jane.

It tasted delicious, too.

"I don't know how you're going to follow this,"

Viv said. "Anything else is sure to be an anti-climax!"

"Don't you be too sure," he chuckled, before putting a CD on to entertain Viv, then disappearing for what felt like hours, though in fact it was only twenty or so minutes.

The main course, when he brought it in, was all one colour: pink. *Very* pink, with odd-looking lumpy bits in. She screwed up her face as she examined it. No, she would have to admit defeat. She hadn't a clue what it was and looked at Shane for an explanation.

"Give up?" he said. "It's Seafood Gumbo, or supposed to be. I think I went a little too mad with the tomato puree. I hope it tastes better than it looks. See, when I said mussels and straw-berries, I wasn't far out. It's prawns and mango instead."

Viv dipped her fork in and took a tiny mouthful. "Ooh, it's really yummy!" she said. "You really are clever. I'm going to make a sexist remark now: I've never met a man who could cook before."

"How about that ex-boyfriend of yours ... Jon, isn't it? Couldn't he cook?"

Viv wished Shane hadn't mentioned Jon's name because, the second he did, she felt as if a dark cloud had drifted through the window and was hovering over the pair of them at the table. Her stomach tensed up, too, and she could hardly eat.

"Not as far as I know," she answered brusquely. "He lived at home and his mum did all the cooking."

"A fatal mistake," Shane said. "Every boy ought

to be taught to cook before he leaves home, same as every girl."

She wanted desperately to defend Jon. She didn't like Shane having anything to criticize him about. She felt a dart of anger towards him which she knew was totally unjustified, so she did her best to dampen it down. Meanwhile Shane was still talking about cooking.

"Who taught you? Your mum?" Viv asked him.

"She and my oldest sister between them. When I was twelve, I cooked the entire Christmas dinner," he said proudly.

"You'll be a really useful husband when you get married," Viv told him. As soon as she'd said it, she felt a fiery flush sweep over her cheeks and she could have bitten off her tongue as a silence fell which was so deep that Viv could hear herself chewing. Why, oh *why*, had she mentioned the word *marriage*? Would Shane think she was dropping some dreadful hint?

He was staring at his plate. Then he looked up and his eyes met hers. "I hope the girl who marries me will want me for a lot more than my cooking ability," he said.

"Oh, I didn't mean... What I meant was—"

"Don't get in a flap! You haven't said anything wrong. I was just thinking, that's all," Shane assured her. His blue eyes crinkled at the outer corners and his lips began to twitch upwards into a smile.

I love it when he smiles, she thought, basking in the radiance that was beaming from him. I love the way his eyes crinkle, I love that tiny dimple in his chin. I love the way his blond hair is almost silver on his temples, and the way his hair is all smooth and shiny just before it goes into a wave. I love him. Hey, I do! I love him!

Viv smiled, too, and their smiles seemed to ignite in the air between them and shimmer there and return to their owners doubled in sheer force of happiness.

Yes, I do, I love him, she thought. Her eyes were pouring her soul into his eyes across their half eaten meals. His went dark for a moment, as if opening to let her into his soul. Then they blazed at her like twin blue flames. I'd always thought blue eyes looked cold, she mused, but Shane's eyes are blue heat. They're burning me up. They—

Her observations were interrupted by Shane clasping her wrist.

"Viv," he murmured. "You look so beautiful. Your eyes have gone golden, like a tiger's. I know our dinners will get cold but right now, there's nothing I want to do more than kiss you."

They rose at the same instant and moved without a word over to the sofa. He took her in his arms lightly, like he did when they danced on the boat. She felt like a piece of thistledown floating within the circle of his embrace. His lips brushed hers like the wings of a butterfly and every bit of her body went hyper-sensitive and tingly.

He breathed on her forehead, blowing away a stray curl. Then he blew warmly and gently into her ear so that she shivered from head to toe. He pulled her in closer to him and the pressure of their arms round one another increased as their kiss grew more passionate. And then they were sinking on to the sofa, still lost in their embrace, and the room spun and the music speeded up and echoed round Viv's head as Shane kissed her more thoroughly and more passionately than she had ever been kissed.

He was shaking like she was. There was a kind of desperate searching in their kiss, a yearning to get closer still, to merge with one another until they were no longer two separate individuals but one whole, complete unit of pure love, two pieces of a jigsaw that exactly fitted.

"I love you, Viv," Shane murmured huskily, his eyelashes fluttering against her eyelids as his nose stroked hers.

"I love you, too," responded Viv in a shaky whisper.

She hadn't meant to tell him that, but it seemed that her heart had spoken for her, overruling her mind and any suspicions about him she might have.

Now that the words were out, and hanging in the air, she seemed to hear the echo of them everywhere, spreading out like ripples from a thrown stone in a lake. Out and out, wider and wider, until one reached Jon and told him of her infidelity. She'd never said "I love you" to anyone else but Jon, until now. She felt as though she had kicked a snowball down a mountain and started an avalanche which she was powerless to stop.

Feeling heavy with the inevitability of it all, she closed her eyes and tilted her lips to Shane's, giving herself up to the love she felt for the boy with the midnight blue eyes.

As they kissed, the dinner he'd cooked with so much care congealed forgotten upon the table, an accidental sacrifice to a love so new, so intense, so incredibly beautiful.

17

Viv was round at Rosie's place. It was Saturday afternoon, a breezy day in March, eight days after that blissful meal at Shane's. The small patio garden was full of yellow daffodils, bright as pieces of the sun, and Viv was standing at Rosie's bedroom window admiring them between the pink curtains.

"Isn't it funny, the way life changes?" Viv said.

Rosie was sitting on her bed, painting her fingernails pearly pink. "How do you mean?" she asked, not daring to look up.

"The way habits change, friendships change, things you've relied on for ages suddenly vanish."

"You're in a serious mood today, aren't you?" Rosie pointed out. "What's brought this on?"

"If you must know, it's Trish. She's ... well, we're just not as close as we used to be. I suppose it's pretty inevitable really. Whatever she may say, I know she'll never approve of me and my two-timing. You're the only person I can really talk to about everything. I feel much closer to you than I do to Trish at the moment."

Rosie gave a wry little grin. "I hope I'm a real friend and not just a Trish substitute," she said.

"Of course you're a real friend. You always have been. Anyone who lets me babble on about my love-life non-stop has to be a good friend. To go back to Trish, though... I'm worried about her, Rosie. Do you think she's ill or anything? Depressed? She always has a sort of anxious look on her face these days."

"Has she? I haven't noticed." Rosie gave her little finger a final dab. "I think she's just swotting hard."

"Like Jon. We had two years of being practically inseparable and seeing each other three or four times a week and always at weekends, and now it's kind of hit and miss, he fits me in between his studying sessions."

"You've got Shane, though," Rosie pointed out, waving a hand in the air to dry.

"In theory, yes," she answered her. "In practice, he's about as elusive as Jon. He's got quite a lot of work to do for his computer course, plus he's got his band. *And* he earns extra cash helping Steve with his disco. Anyway, he's away for a few days now, gone to see his family in Cheshire. He'll be back on Wednesday and we've got a date then. But for now I'm all alone! Abandoned! Nobody wants me!"

"I want you right now to help me with this homework. Can you translate that bit there, the part I've highlighted?" Rosie requested, pointing a gleaming fingernail at the book on her bedroom carpet.

"I heard something funny the other day," Viv said. "Fiona told me that when she did the oral part of her French exam, they asked her what *La voiture est sur le chemin* meant."

"The car is on the road, isn't it?" said Rosie.

"Yes, but guess what Fiona said? She translated it as *the vulture is sitting on the chimney*! No wonder she failed!"

The two of them howled with mirth, in the course of which Rosie knocked the bottle of nail varnish over. It went all over her pillow and she dashed to the bathroom and fetched back a large plastic bottle of varnish remover and started dabbing it all over the pillow-case with a piece of cotton-wool.

"Pooh! The room stinks." Viv coughed and flung the window open. "That's better. Now, where we we?"

"Talking about men, of course. Wilson's taking me to that new American burger place tonight. You can hang out there and they show American rock videos on a big screen on the wall."

"I'm not going anywhere," Viv said dolefully. "Perhaps I'll give Trish a ring."

"I wouldn't bother if I were you," Rosie said. "She won't be in."

"How do you know?"

Rosie hesitated slightly, then replied vaguely, "Oh, she mentioned something about going to a concert. With her sister, I think she said."

"Why does she never think of asking *me* if I'd

like to go?" Viv said in hurt tones. "Once upon a time, we used to go through the local paper together and mark all the things we wanted to go to."

"She probably thinks you're too busy these days," Rosie pointed out. "And most of the time it's true, isn't it?"

"Yes, I suppose so. I can quite see that she might feel left out. But she never even tells me what's going on with Mike, or how she feels. Does she tell you?"

"Mm," Rosie murmured absently. She got up and began tidying the cosmetics on her dressing table. Then she popped a cassette into her machine and the room was suddenly filled with the strains of Viv's un-favourite band.

"I can see you're trying to give me a hint," Viv said. She stood up and reached for her jacket.

"No, you don't have to go yet. I'll put something else on instead," said Rosie, pressing the Off button on the cassette deck.

"You've got to get ready for Wilson. I've got to get ready for –" Viv paused and placed the back of her hand against her forehead, in the melo-dramatic way beloved of actresses in old black and white films – "for a fantastic night in on my own, boo-hoo!"

Rosie made a rude noise. "About the only night you *have* been in lately."

Viv thought of all the nights she'd stayed in fretting and worrying. No, she wasn't going to have a moan about that. She was the girl who'd struck doubly lucky, after all.

She said goodbye to Rosie and as she left, a sudden impulse made her turn and walk in the opposite direction to home. She would go and see Trish, see if she could have one of the happy, gossipy sessions they used to have, before Trish went out to wherever she was going. Perhaps she could go to the concert with Trish and her sister, if they hadn't already bought tickets.

Trish lived in a big block of flats called Arundel Court, on the sixth floor. Viv went up to the heavy steel door and pressed numbers two and six on the complicated intercom system.

"Yes?" the voice of Trish's mother crackled through the amplifier behind the metal grille.

"It's Viv."

"*Who?*"

"*Viv!*" she yelled.

"Sorry, I can hardly hear you. The intercom's on the blink. Trish isn't in, I'm afraid, dear."

"Do you know when she'll be back?" bellowed Viv.

"No, dear. She's gone out with that boyfriend of hers. I don't expect her back till late."

"You mean Mike?"

"What did you say, dear?"

"*MIKE!*" shrieked Viv.

"Haven't seen him for a long time, dear."

"Oh," said Viv, her eyes wide with speculation. "Tell her I called. 'Bye."

Viv's brain was buzzing. She couldn't wait to phone Rosie, though it would have to wait till tomorrow now as Rosie would be out. She rang Rosie on Sunday morning. "Hm, that's interesting,"

Rosie said, then went on to talk about her date the previous evening. It didn't strike Viv at the time, but thinking about it later – *much* later – she realized that Rosie could have sounded a bit more curious. It was almost as if she were evading the whole issue...

With Jon presumably working, though it wasn't like him not to have phoned to say hello at least, and Shane in Macclesfield visiting his mother, Viv got an awful lot of homework done including a German essay she'd been putting off for ages. She imagined poor Jon slumped over a table piled high with books, and Shane sitting talking with his mother and sisters. She imagined two young women in their twenties, as blonde as he was, and they were all looking at old family photographs and swopping intimate reminiscences. She wished she could be there, too, to hear anecdotes about his childhood and find out more about him.

On Monday, Trish was off school with a sore throat. ("Too much snogging," joked Viv to Rosie.) By the end of that evening, she still hadn't heard from Jon, and she was feeling quite agitated. Was he ill? Twice, she had picked up the receiver to call him, but pride had stopped her. Surely, no matter how hard he was studying, or how foul he felt, he could pick up the phone and speak to her, if only for ten minutes?

On Tuesday, Trish was back. Viv was chatting to Rosie in the corridor when she went to sidle past them, a couple of books under her arm.

"You're not getting away that easily," Viv said.

"Come on, now, own up, tell us all about him."

"All about who?"

"Him. He who you were out with on Saturday night. He who presumably gave you the bad throat. You know ... *him*."

Trish went a bit pale and her expression was completely deadpan. "I don't know what you're talking about," she said haughtily.

Rosie was standing there saying nothing. Viv glanced at her for encouragement. "Your mum said Mike was no longer in the picture, so come on, own up, who are you seeing now? You're not ashamed of him or something, are you? It's Phil Castelli, isn't it?"

Trish remained silent, which Viv took as assent. She smiled at Trish. "That's great! I hope it's going really well between you. I want to hear all about it. We both do, don't we, Rosie?"

Rosie nodded.

"Well, must dash, I'll be late for History," Trish said. "See you."

"Now we know!" Viv said to Rosie. But there was no time to continue the conversation because just then Irmgard Schmidt, the young German language assistant, walked briskly down the corridor towards them and shooed them into the classroom.

At lunchbreak Viv looked for Trish but she was nowhere to be found. Rosie, too, had absented herself. She'd said she was going to the school library, but when Viv peeped in, there was no sign of her anywhere.

"Abandoned again!" she sighed dramatically to

145

herself outside the library door. "An orphan, a foundling, alone against the elements."

"What was that, Vivienne?" enquired Janet Hayes, the art teacher, coming across her in the corridor.

"Er ... nothing, just reciting some Shakespeare to myself, doing some A-level practice."

"Very good, Vivienne, but it would be better if you did it somewhere else. People are trying to work in here."

"Yes, Miss Hayes," she said. She trudged off to the cloakroom muttering, "Nobody loves me, everybody hates me."

She was by no means alone in there. There was a constant bustle of girls putting on or hanging up coats and going to and from the toilets. Her hand was just reaching towards the peg for her navy mac when she heard Rosie's voice.

"Seeing Jon tonight?"

She spun round, the word "No" already formed on her lips. And that's when she saw that Rosie's question hadn't been directed at her. She was talking to Trish...

18

Both girls went ashen when they saw Viv standing there. For a few paralysed moments, nothing was said. It was as if they had all been frozen in the positions they happened to be in.

Viv was the first to move. Her knees crumpled and she sank on to the ledge beneath the coat pegs, where people left their wellingtons and muddy boots. The room was spinning and she felt faint. Her heart felt as if it was fluttering in her chest instead of beating. She put her head down between her knees – and when she finally felt well enough to look up, only Rosie was there. Rosie, looking most concerned and exceedingly guilty. Of Trish, there wasn't a sign.

"So now you know," Rosie said. "I'm sorry you had to find out this way."

It took Viv several attempts to get her vocal cords to work, but finally she croaked, "How … how long has this been going on?"

Rosie gave a rueful grimace. "A few weeks."

"So when Jon met me in The Pier last week and was so extra attentive and loving, it wasn't anything to do with feeling bad because he'd been neglecting me for his work, it was just pure guilt because of what he'd been getting up to behind my back!" Even as she said it, she reflected that she hadn't a leg to stand on. He'd only been doing what she herself had been doing. But at the moment she felt much too hurt to analyse her own behaviour.

"I suppose so," Rosie admitted.

"You knew on Saturday and you didn't tell me. How *could* you?" Tears welled up in Viv's eyes and *Nobody loves me, everybody hates me* wandered into her head like a mocking chant.

"How could Jon have brought me flowers and kissed me like he did, when all the time he knew damn well he was two-timing me with Trish? With my best friend! *Ex*-best friend, now!" she finished savagely.

"Er, excuse me saying so, but it's rather a case of the pot calling the kettle black, isn't it?" Rosie ventured.

Viv glared at her and half rose and Rosie took a hasty step back. "Look, Viv – we've got a class now and we're late, as usual. Come round to my place tonight and I promise I'll tell you everything I know," she said.

"Well, there's no point in going round to Trish's. Not if she's seeing Jon. No point going to his, either. So I suppose you'll have to do. To think I trusted you... Trusted you both!" Viv said bitterly. She wiped her eyes and blew her nose and followed Rosie to the classroom, but she felt as if she were in another world ... another universe.

There was no lingering on the way home from school that day. Viv went straight round to Rosie's. They went up to her bedroom and Viv firmly closed the door and turned round, grim-faced, ready to begin her interrogation.

All through her classes that afternoon her brain had been whirling. Jon ... the only boy she'd ever trusted! And Trish, her best friend... She would never be able to trust anybody again. What did Shane really get up to on the nights he didn't see her? Maybe he had half a dozen groupies stowed away all over town! That saying, "love is blind," certainly was true.

"Right then," she snapped. "Tell all! When did this begin. And how?"

"It was after you told Trish that you were seeing Shane on the side. She's always had a thing about Jon, you know that. She thinks he's fantastic. She's always been jealous of you going out with him, and when she heard that you were two-timing him, she felt really sorry for him. You'd told her how keen on Shane you were. Trish said it sounded as if you were going off Jon and it was only a matter of time before you split up."

"So she made a pass at him?"

"Well, sort of. She arranged to bump into him outside his college, sort of accidentally on purpose. Then she suggested they went for a drink together and – well, you know how persuasive she can be when she gets going. You know what a flirt she is. We've all seen her when she swings into action. No boy stands a chance. Well, she is very pretty, isn't she?"

"Yes, but we're not bad, Rosie!" Viv said hotly. "So then what happened?"

"She said she knew you two weren't seeing so much of each other lately. I think she worked on him psychologically, made him think you were going off him."

"Did she tell him about Shane?"

"I don't think she's that much of a bitch, Viv. I think you can trust her not to go that far. She certainly hasn't told *me* that she's told him."

"But he was so wonderful when I saw him the other night! I quite fell in love with him all over again. When he kissed me, I felt every tiny bit of the kiss, and all its reactions, just like I used to... Just like I do with Shane."

"So you *were* falling out of love with Jon?" It was Rosie's turn to quiz Viv now.

Viv sank down on to Rosie's bedroom chair with its big, fat, patchwork cushion. She heaved a great, shuddering sigh. "I don't know," she admitted tearfully. "I still loved him, but we'd got into a sort of rut, always going to the movies on a certain night, always going for walks at weekends... It must have been getting a bit boring, or I wouldn't have found Shane so exciting.

"I suppose we were taking each other for granted. When I really think of it, we'd been more like brother and sister for ages. Except for when he kissed me. That never lost its magic," she confessed ruefully. "I still fancy him like hell. But

... it had got to be a habit. Maybe he felt the same."

She suddenly remembered the odd remark Jon had made on their way back from the zoo, about being good friends. At the time, she'd challenged him about it, but now she realized he was probably right. What's more, he was probably contrasting the new feelings he had for Trish with the old, set-in-their-ways ones he had for her.

"Do you think Jon's fallen in love with Trish?" she asked Rosie.

"Well, Trish is certainly madly in love with him. That's why she's been avoiding you."

"Jon loves Trish, Trish loves Jon, Jon feels guilty about me, Trish feels guilty about me, I love Shane, I feel guilty about Jon, I hate Trish." Viv paused, thinking about this complicated set-up.

Then she raised her head and gave Rosie a steady, clear-eyed look. "No, I don't hate Trish," she said solemnly. "And I don't hate Jon, either. I forgive them both, because don't you see what they've done? They've left the way clear for me to go out with Shane, without having to feel any guilt, without having to dodge and hide and be careful what I say to everyone."

She gave a smile which started as a brave quiver of the lips and quickly developed into a wide grin.

"It couldn't be better, really, could it?" She laughed, bounced out of her chair and grabbed the surprised Rosie's arms and danced her round the bedroom floor. "I feel so happy now!" she cried. "Really, really happy! Everything's straightforward again. I'm in love with Shane and there's nothing in the way of it. I feel as though the whole future is stretching ahead of me and the sun's shining."

"Steady on!" said Rosie, who'd tripped on the rug and nearly fallen. "Don't get too carried away..."

"Why not? Shane loves me, he's said so, I love him, I know I do... That's all we need. Oh Rosie, it's going to be so wonderful!"

Shane rang the moment she got back home. She was still elated and bubbly and his good timing just added fuel to her conviction that everything was going to work out perfectly.

"I've really missed you," he said. "Sorry I couldn't phone you from up there. I just didn't get a moment, what with Mum and sisters and nieces and nephews – I seemed to be on the go all the time. I really am sorry. I've missed you a lot. I'm so glad to be back. I can't wait to see you."

"I'm dying to see you, too." Viv was aware of the eagerness in her voice. There seemed no point in trying to hide it when they both felt the same way.

It was wonderful feeling free to kiss Shane on her own doorstep, to walk down her street holding hands with him. She skipped like a child all the way to his van.

"What's got into you tonight?" Shane asked laughingly.

"I haven't seen you for ages and I'd forgotten how it felt," she said.

His answer was to swing her off her feet and

twirl her round in his arms. He kissed her, then opened the van door and lifted her in. "Where to?" he asked. "Your chariot awaits!"

She remembered the place where she'd had such a great time on her last – her *very* last, as it had turned out – date with Jon. She examined her feelings to see if the thought of going there again so soon caused her any pain. It didn't.

"Let's go to The Pier," she said.

It was packed out and they couldn't get a seat. She didn't see anyone she knew in there so they decided to go somewhere else.

"I know. I'll take you to see the club where we're playing on Saturday. It's our biggest gig yet," Shane said.

They drove right out of town and into the country. When Shane turned the van into a scrunchy gravel driveway, Viv gasped as she caught a glimpse of what lay at the end of it.

"It's a palace!" she cried.

"It's The Turrets Country Club. A bit of all right, isn't it?"

"Do you think they'll let us in? I'm not exactly dressed for a place like this," said Viv, grimacing down at her jeans and the tan leather jacket which had been a Christmas present from her parents.

"Neither am I. But I'm sure they'll let us have a drink at the bar even if we can't go in the main room. They've got two bars there, one in the room where the music and dancing takes place and another more casual one where you can get snacks and play darts. I'll have a word with the manager, say I'm a member of the band that's playing there tomorrow and I've come to check the electric plugs and work out where we're going to place the equipment on the stage. I'm sure he'll let us in. It's early, after all. There won't be many punters there yet."

Sure enough, when they got there and asked to speak to the manager, he and Shane exchanged a few words and they were let in, after they'd made a promise to be out in half an hour when the evening's cabaret act was due to start.

"That's a bit mean of him, isn't it?" Shane grumbled. He put an arm around Viv and hugged her to him. "Still, at least you'll get a chance to see the place – and you'll be able to spend all evening here free on Saturday."

She gazed up at him, her eyes glowing with love. "I can't wait," she said.

They had a drink in the main bar, which was sumptuous in the extreme, with deep red and cream marble and burnished brass. On the way home, when they were still deep in the countryside, Shane turned into a little lane and stopped the van.

"Viv?" he said breathlessly. "I've been dying to do this all night. I can't wait any longer." He pulled her against him, enveloping her in his arms and delivering a crushing kiss on to her open, eager lips.

The kiss was broken off all too soon because the hump of the engine cover, which was burning hot, and the sticking-out gears got in their way.

Shane wound down the window and stuck his

hand out. "It's not raining or anything and it's not too cold. Fancy a walk?" he suggested.

"Yes, if my legs will hold me up after that kiss," she said.

He jumped out of the van, came round to her side and gently lifted her down, pressing his lips to hers and not taking them away even after her feet had met the ground.

"Oh, Shane..." she whispered. "I feel all giddy after that."

With their arms wrapped around each other's waists, they walked slowly down the dark lane. A moth flew into Viv's face and made her jump and splutter. Shane laughed. They came to a stile leading to a footpath which skirted the edge of a field. Shane helped Viv to clamber over.

It was muddy in the field and Viv was glad of the ankleboots she had on. The night was completely silent and still, no breeze to stir the leafless branches or make the hedgerows rustle.

"Listen," Shane said. "What can you hear?"

Viv listened. "Nothing," she replied.

"That's just it – nothing. Isn't it wonderful? You never get this in town, there's always a car, or voices, or a neighbour's television, or a police siren. You never get this deep, thick silence. It's so quiet, you can almost drink it."

He opened his mouth and took a great lungful of air. Viv did the same. It tasted fresh and good.

"On nights like this, you really feel part of Nature, don't you?" he said. "We could be the first – the only – man and woman on Earth. Do you know what I mean?"

"Yes." Viv spoke softly, not wanting to disturb the tranquillity or break the spell.

"It's magic, isn't it? Sheer magic. Just look at those stars!"

Viv followed his gaze and saw that the sky, which she had thought dark and covered in cloud, was in fact luminous with stars which shed a frosty, bluey-silver light over the fields. She could make out the rise of a hill, the silhouettes of bushes and trees, all outlined in an almost phosphorescent glow.

"It's so beautiful," she whispered. "I'm so glad you brought me here."

Very gently Shane turned her round to face him. "I'm so much in love with you, Viv," he said, in a voice thick with emotion. "I don't know what it is you do to me, but I'm a complete goner. I'm yours, you know... You can do what you want with me. I just completely melt and go to pieces when you're around."

Viv had been going to speak, to tell him she loved him, too, but the words caught in her throat and she felt like crying. No boy had ever expressed such open love for her. Jon had never said things like this to her. He'd told her he loved her a thousand times, but had never gone into details about how she made him feel. Before this, she'd had no idea about how boys' emotions worked. Why, they felt things just like girls did, really. Their feelings went just as deep, they got just as carried away.

She was so affected by his words that she couldn't say anything for a while. She just stood there, letting Shane put his arms around her.

"You're shivering. Are you cold?" he asked, concern in his voice.

"No ... no. I'm just ... oh, I don't know."

He put his hand up and touched her face to steer her lips to his, then immediately removed his fingers from her cheek.

"Your face is wet. You're not crying, are you?"

Viv's trembling body started to shake in earnest and she collapsed against him, sobbing on his shoulder, all the tension and worry of the last few weeks pouring out of her.

"Viv ... Viv darling ... what's wrong? Please tell me." Shane hugged her against him, stroking her hair.

At last, she was able to straighten up. In the glow from the stars, she could just see his face, make out the gleam of his eyes as they gazed so anxiously into hers. She gave a little, wobbly smile.

"I'm OK," she said. "I'm crying because I'm happy, not because I'm sad. You see, I've never loved anyone like this before, and I'm just ... so ... happy!"

19

Trish was waiting for Viv by the school gates.

"Tina gave me your message," she said. She looked a bit fearful. "Do you *really* not mind about me and Jon? I didn't set out to steal him off you, you know, I just felt sorry for him. We've always got on well. It just sort of ... happened."

"Hmm," Viv grunted dubiously. Despite what she'd told Trish's sister Tina the previous night, she wasn't going to forgive all *that* easily. "But you might have waited until I'd plucked up courage to finish with Jon. It would have felt better. I do feel I need to talk to him about it ... explain a few things."

"He wants to talk to you, too," Trish said. "He says he'd like to see you tonight if you're not doing anything. He's going to ring you when you get in. Well, I ... I'd better be going, I suppose."

"Yes." Viv made no attempt to walk into school with Trish, but let her go on ahead, alone. She knew that as far as sinning was concerned, she was far worse than Trish, but nevertheless, the way Trish had gone about it still rankled. She had *trusted* Trish.

But Jon trusted you, nagged the voice of her conscience...

Jon said he'd like to meet Viv for a drink, as they would get no privacy at his home or hers and parental tongues would wag. They chose a small pub on the corner of a street close to where Viv lived.

The Coach and Horses wasn't at all trendy, its clientele being mainly elderly men nursing pints of Guinness and their equally elderly dogs. But it had the virtue of being quiet and of being somewhere where nobody who knew them was likely to come up and interrupt their heart-to-heart.

Viv deliberately walked in ten minutes late. Jon was sitting at a table near the door with a pint glass of lager in front of him. He looked very sheepish.

"Um, hello," he gulped, refusing to meet her eye.

"Don't worry, I won't bite you," Viv said. She walked up to the bar and ordered a grapefruit juice and Jon leapt up to pay for it, but she wouldn't let him.

She sat down, steeling herself, knowing that, in order to clear the air thoroughly, she was going to have to tell him about Shane. She wasn't going to enjoy Jon finding out that she had been just as deceitful as he had been.

His hand reached across the table towards hers, faltered, and found its way back to his lap again. "I keep forgetting..." he said.

"Forgetting what?" Viv was quite enjoying her moment of being the wronged woman. After all, it *would* only be a moment; it would stop the second she confessed and he discovered he was more wronged than she was. Or maybe they were equal.

"That we're not going out any more."

"Friends can still touch each other's hands, can't they?" Viv gave him a provocative look. Stop it, she told herself sternly. Don't play games with him, it's not fair.

"Look, Jon, I've got something I'd better tell you. Cards on the table time." She hesitated, drawing a deep breath before telling him the bitter truth. "I … well, I've got somebody else, too."

Jon looked shocked. "That was quick work!"

"Not as quick as all that. It's been going on for some time."

"Oh?" Jon frowned. "How long exactly?" he enquired frostily.

Viv bit her lip and knew that her guilt was showing now. "Um … since … well, since Fiona's party, to be precise." Now it was her turn to look sheepishly downwards.

"I don't believe it! How could you? But things were still OK between us then!" he exclaimed, anger and hurt in his voice. "Anyway, how could you have met anyone at the party? You were with me all night."

"We just got talking. It was when you were getting the drinks … when we were eating. And later, when I went to the loo, I ran into him as I was coming back to find you and he asked me out."

Now it was Viv who reached for Jon's hand, which was clenched on the tabletop, but he moved it as if her touch had scalded him.

"Please believe me," she begged. "It was a terribly hard decision to make. I really suffered and lost sleep over it."

"I should bloody well think so!" he snapped. His lips were tight, his face pale and his eyes narrowed in an angrier expression than she had ever seen him produce. She cringed slightly, then ploughed on.

"It was meant to be just one date, out of curiosity. But he was really nice and things got a bit out of hand. I kept telling myself each time was going to be the last. Was it like that with you and Trish?"

"I don't want to talk about it," he said.

"Fair's fair! I'm being open and honest with *you*!" she shouted and an old spaniel beneath the next table started growling. "Anyway," she continued, lowering her voice, "you seemed to be going off me, so—"

"What do you mean, going off you? I've got a lot of work to do. That's genuine!"

The spaniel growled again. Viv turned round. "Sorry," she said to its owner, who grunted and went on reading his newspaper.

"I was not going off you," Jon insisted. "I thought you were going off me. But, there again..." He sighed and gave a little shrug before concluding, "...perhaps we had got into a bit of a rut. Let's be honest, things weren't as exciting between us as they used to be, were they?"

"No, they weren't," Viv agreed. "Where does it leave us now?"

"Friends, I hope," Jon said, raising his glass to his lips. He put it down without touching a drop. "Anyway, things were bound to come to a head when I went off to university. We'd have had to make some decisions then. I couldn't see you waiting around for three years till I got my degree. And I mightn't have come home even then. Or I might have met somebody else there. Who knows? Perhaps this has happened for the best."

"Yes, maybe," Viv owned.

"Let's drink to a lifelong friendship."

Jon raised his glass again and Viv raised hers and clinked it against his. "To our friendship," she said.

She felt very warm towards him, very fond of him as they left the pub after one more drink. She had told him a little about Shane, he had said one or two things about Trish and, she decided, it felt OK. She even felt a little sorry for Trish, thinking about Jon's speech about what was likely to happen when he went away to university.

When they got near her house, Jon stopped. "I want to ask you something, Viv," he said.

"What's that?"

"Would you consider giving me just one kiss, for old times' sake?"

"Of course!" Viv took a step towards him. Jon put his arms round her and she raised hers and gave him a cuddle. Strange, she thought, I feel nothing. Nothing at all. And when his lips met hers in a dry, almost wistful kiss, she still felt nothing.

"Thanks," he said, taking his arms away from her.

They both stood awkwardly, facing each other. Suddenly, he grabbed her and crushed her against him and rained kisses on her hair, her forehead, her face, her chin, and finally her lips, which his lips clung to as his whole body strained and trembled against hers.

Viv was gasping for breath when he released her. He cleared his throat and sounded all chokey as he said, "Thanks for two wonderful years, Fluffy-head."

Viv felt tears welling up and spilling down her cheeks. This was the very last time she would ever hear him call her by that familiar nickname. "Good luck, Jon," she said chokily.

He made no reply. He looked as overcome with emotion as she was.

Then she went in. It was over.

Later that evening, she tried to ring Shane. She was desperate to talk to him, desperate to erase the memories of the past and remind herself of that bright future she'd glimpsed the previous night. The phone rang and rang. He was out.

Probably rehearsing for tomorrow night, she thought. Her mournful heart gladdened a little at the thought of going to the fabulous Turrets Club the following evening.

She recalled the starlit walk she had taken with him and her heart swelled with love. She tried to picture Jon's face and it seemed blurred and getting smaller, as if receding down a long tunnel. When she pictured Shane, she saw his eyes, his smile, his long, unruly fair hair as clearly as if he were standing right in front of her.

"I love you, Shane," she said out loud to her bedroom wall. "I love you." She tried to project the words into space, saw them cross the night sky like a banner drawn by a plane and hover over his roof, then disappear through his window. "I love you," she repeated and mentally gave the words a last little push, straight into his mind.

There, she thought; he knows now, he can't have any doubts. If he's at all tuned in to me, he knows.

20

When it got to eight o'clock the next evening and she still hadn't heard from Shane, Viv was in torment. There was no reply from his number – she'd tried it five times. It was too late now for him to come and pick her up, but he hadn't told her where they should meet, or whether he was expecting her to make her own way to The Turrets because he was going with the band in the van.

"Shane, *Shane*," she muttered through tightly clenched teeth. "For God's sake call me, just *call* me."

But the telephone stayed silent.

He'd told her that they would be playing their first set at nine. She would have to leave right away if she was to stand any chance of being there for the start.

She had stared at her father's big road atlas time and time again and the location of the club was imprinted on her memory. Bus to the station, train to Fetherley, then a taxi to the club. At least she could rely on getting a lift back as there would be no trains running by the time *Bombshell* had finished their second set.

Something had to have happened for him not to have rung. Maybe the van's broken down and they're having to rush around hiring another one, she thought. Or perhaps someone's had their guitar or drum kit stolen. Or maybe one of the band is ill and they're desperately looking for a substitute musician. It had to be an emergency; there was no other explanation of why Shane would neglect to contact her. Especially now that they were so much in love.

She was particularly upset that this should have happened tonight, of all nights – tonight, when she wanted to celebrate her new-found freedom to love him as he deserved. She had put on the red dress he liked so much. She knew she was looking particularly attractive – or would do if there wasn't such a worried frown on her face.

At ten past eight she set out alone. Trains to Fetherley ran every half hour and she got to the station to find she had twenty minutes to wait.

Fortunately, there was a line of taxis queueing up outside Fetherley station so she had no difficulty in getting to the club. She walked up the wide flight of steps to the entrance feeling the familiar flutter of excitement start up inside her at the thought of seeing Shane.

It was twenty past nine. They would be playing now. He would be worrying about her, wondering if she'd make it. She imagined the smile that would transform his face when he saw her ... the way those midnight blue eyes would sparkle into hers.

"Excuse me, miss, may I see your ticket?" A uniformed commissionaire was blocking her route across the foyer.

"I'm on the guest list. I'm Viv McCulloch, the girlfriend of Shane Russell, the bass player," Viv confidently informed him.

The man went over to the desk and lifted a sheet of paper off it. He scanned it slowly, then shook his head.

"I'm sorry, but your name's not here," he said.

"Oh!" Viv's confidence drained out of her in one second flat. She felt cold all over. "But ... but I don't understand! He *must* have put it on... Unless another member of the band wrote out the list and forgot me," she said.

"Sorry, I can't let you in if your name's not down here," the man said pompously.

"Look, I came here with him just two nights ago. Someone must have seen me. The manager!" she exclaimed in a flash of inspiration. "He talked to us. Is he here? I'm sure he'd remember me."

"George?" the commissionaire called to another man behind the desk. "See if Eddie's in his office, will you?"

The man went off and Viv crossed her fingers. Please, please let him be there and let him remember me, she prayed.

Her prayer was answered, though not quite as pleasantly as she had hoped, when George came back with Eddie, the manager, who leered and said, "Oh, let the girlie in, will you? We can always do with a few more pretty young women about the place."

Viv fumed, but she didn't show it, just smiled sweetly and said, "Thanks," then swept past the officious comissionaire and down the corridor to the glass doors which led into the club's main hall.

She could hear the pounding beat while she was still in the foyer. As she entered the room, she was almost deafened. A few people were dancing, but most were sitting around at tables, and scarlet-clad waiters and waitresses were bustling around with trays of drinks and snacks.

Coloured spotlights played on the stage. The lead singer was at full throttle. Shane was standing next to him, bending backwards as he plucked the strings of his bass in a funky style, pulling them as hard as he could, then letting them snap back on to the metal frets of the guitar neck. She was relieved to see him. At least nothing had happened to him, though there was still a mystery to be solved.

Viv found a seat as close to the front as she could, though it had the disadvantage of placing her ears rather too close to the bank of amplifiers. The tables were in semi-gloom. Would Shane be able to see her?

A waiter came over and asked her what she wanted.

"A white wine spritzer, please," she said. She loved wine mixed with fizzy mineral water; it diluted the flavour of the kind of cheap, over-dry wine they normally served in pubs and bars and was more thirst-quenching, as well as allowing you to drink more without getting drunk. And tonight, her instincts told her, she would be well advised to keep her head as she had to find some way of letting Shane know she was here.

She tried willing him to look her way but though once or twice his eyes seemed to be scanning the room, they failed to stop at her table. She tried giving him a wave, but he didn't see that, either. So she resigned herself to having to wait to the end of their set and then going backstage to find him.

The song finished and another, quieter one started. Shane stepped forward to a microphone and sang harmony vocals with the lead singer. Viv leant her elbows on the table, rested her chin on her interlaced fingers and relaxed, entranced by the song which bore all the hallmarks of having been written by Shane.

After they had finished and the applause had died down, Shane put down his bass and picked up an acoustic six-string guitar which Viv recognized as the one he had played *Mirage* on when he had sung to her in his flat.

"What you just heard was a song I wrote two years ago," he told the audience. "Now I'd like to play you something a bit more up-to-date. This one isn't two years old, nor two months, nor even two weeks. I started it just two days ago and finished it this morning. The band haven't heard it yet, which is why you're going to have to put up with just me and my guitar."

Is it about me? thought Viv. Is it a love song he's written about Wednesday night? She felt a glow of warm anticipation steal over her and fixed her eyes on Shane.

He plucked the first few notes and she became instantly aware, from the minor key and the expression on his face, that she wasn't in for a happy love song. It sounded more like a lament. Could it be that someone he was close to had died since Wednesday? His grandmother? His mother, even? A friend?

Once he started singing the words, however, the event the song was celebrating was made clear, though it made no sense to Viv.

"I caught a glimpse of Paradise
I saw blue waters shine,
I caught a kiss and smile from you
And thought that they were mine.
I didn't think of past mistakes,
I didn't think at all,
Just stepped out on the edge of love
Heading for a fall.

Two-timer, you've broken my heart,
Your words of love were a poisoned dart.
Two-timer, I'm falling apart,
Wind this video back to the start."

What is he on about? fretted Viv. Did one of his old girlfriends come back out of the past and remind him of why they split up? It must have been a really powerful and unhappy experience to make him write something as sad and angry as this.

There were two more verses and when he sung the final line of the chorus for the very last time, he stopped playing and sang unaccompanied in a slow, hoarse, whispery voice that tore at Viv's heart. She wanted to rush up on to the stage and hold him in her arms and tell him that everything was OK and she was here now and she loved him. She would do anything in her power to erase that anguished look from his face and make him smile again, bring back to his eyes the lovelight that had shone from them last Wednesday.

As he was putting down his guitar, he spoke a few hoarse, emotional words into the microphone. "If there are any two-timers in the audience tonight, I hope they'll realize that they can't go round breaking people's hearts without getting their own broken, too." And, for the first time that evening, he stared directly at Viv.

She rose in her seat and opened her mouth, but nothing came out except a strangled gasp. She felt as if he'd pointed a gun at her and shot her.

Someone's told him about Jon... The words sank like gloomy stones through the thick mud that her brain had turned into. Someone had told him and it was so unfair! Just as she had become free to love him and him alone, her past had caught up with her.

Suddenly, she couldn't stand being in the room where she had been so shamed. She stood up so quickly and clumsily that her chair fell over, but she didn't stop to pick it up, just stumbled blindly between the tables, like someone who was drunk, pushed open the glass doors and ran down the corridor.

Her first thought was to find Shane and tell him the truth. But he would be with the rest of the band and anyway, how could she get him to believe her? Besides, if she had a scene with him here, it might ruin the second half of the show because he'd be too upset to play properly.

I'll write to him, she thought. I'll write him a really long letter telling him the truth about everything, and I'll tell him how much I love him and that he's the most important thing in my life. I'll put it through his door first thing in the morning. He'll get it as soon as he wakes up. He'll read it and ring me and I'll see him and everything will be all right.

All the way home she hoped – longed – for her imagined scenario to come true.

She sat up half the night writing to him, crumpling pages up and throwing them away until her carpet was littered with screwed-up balls of paper. She was trying to tell Shane that she wasn't a coldhearted, calculating two-timer any more, that it was over with Jon, that she really, really loved him. But it was difficult, so difficult, to say it right, to sound sincere and not like a guilty individual trying to cover up her wrongdoings.

At last she felt she'd got it right, and she folded up the sheet of paper, sealed it into an envelope and set her alarm clock for seven a.m. This unheard-of hour was the earliest she had ever got up on a Sunday but, with the greatest love of her

life at stake, she would have got up at five if there
had been a bus then. In fact, she felt like walking
to Marsden End right then, but she was far too
exhausted.

Oh, Shane, she thought as she lay down to try
and catch some sleep, please believe me. Please
forgive me. I would never knowingly hurt you. I
love you... As she closed her eyes, two big tears
squeezed from beneath her eyelids and trickled
down her cheeks and made damp marks on her
pillow – stains which had widened and spread by
the time she had cried herself to sleep.

21

It was just over a week later when Viv broke down in Assembly and started sobbing. It was after Sheena Saha, a tiny, angelically pretty third former with a fluting voice, had given the daily reading. This week was devoted to poetry and today's had been *All That's Past* by Walter De La Mare and the last four lines brought home to Viv the minuteness of her problems compared to the vastness of the universe and made her feel how utterly futile life – and especially love – were.

The last line mentioned "fields of amaranth". She hadn't a clue what amaranth was but she imagined it as a blue flower the colour of Shane's eyes and pictured him lying dead amongst the blooms, his eyes closed. Then she thought about Jon, and the full weight of everything she had lost with the ending of the relationship overwhelmed her and tears streamed down her face. She couldn't find a hanky and had to wipe her eyes with her sleeve, and it was her loud sniffing all the way through the Head's announcements that made Trish, who was in the row in front, turn round and give her a look of sympathy and concern.

Trish was waiting for her in the corridor as she trudged sadly back to their classroom. "Have you heard from him yet?" Trish asked.

Viv shook her head. She knew she looked an absolute wreck; pale, with eyes which were red-rimmed from weeping, and blue shadows beneath them as deep as bruises.

"I'm really sorry," Trish said. "It doesn't seem fair that I'm so happy now and you're so miserable."

Viv was too choked with misery to answer and she let Trish put a supportive arm around her shoulders and give her a friendly hug.

"I've got something to tell you that will interest you, though it's a pity I only found out last night," Trish said. "Remember what I said about Sandra?"

Viv's insides gave a lurch.

"Jon and I met her sister, Carla, and her boyfriend at The Pier last night and she told me Sandra had got married. To the boyfriend whose baby it was."

Viv felt as if she was about to be sick. "Who was he?" she managed to whisper.

Trish, perhaps realizing what misery her prolonging of the story was putting Viv through, quickly said, "It wasn't your Shane, so you can stop worrying about that. It was another Shane, a guy called Shane Cousins. He's an electrician and they met at a rave in Walsall. He plays bass in a band. When I heard that it was a Shane who had fair hair and played the guitar, well, you can understand why I jumped to the obvious conclusion. I'm really sorry. Oh – heads down, here comes Jim-and-Tonic. He's walking as though he's had a few already!"

Viv couldn't believe that there had been no response to her letter. She had lost count of the number of times she had rung him. She had been round to his house twice and rung the bell and hammered on the door, but had had no reply. There was no sign of his van outside, either.

The previous day, she had sneaked out of school early and gone to wait outside his college. But by eight o'clock in the evening, she had given up and gone home. Maybe he was feeling so fed up that he had gone back up North to his mother's, she reasoned. Perhaps he'd gone before she'd delivered her letter and it was still sitting there in the hall, waiting for him to return.

If he ever did...

As she plodded home that afternoon, the weather mocked her. The wind had turned warm and the tulips and daffodils which nodded in people's gardens were like bright jewels glowing in the spring sun. A howling, sleety blizzard would have suited her mood better.

She turned her key in the lock and trudged indoors. Neither of her parents was back from work yet. Some mail had arrived and was sitting on the carpet inside the door. Viv bent to pick it up. Electricity bill, addressed to her father;

something for her mother, looked like her aunt's writing. And what was this funny postcard? It had a boring picture on the front of a redbrick building and a car park. She turned it over. The untidy scrawl on it looked as though it had been written either by a child just learning to write, or by an old person with a shaky hand.

However, it was addressed to her, in different writing, the letters of which were firm and neat and printed. She sank down on to the bottom stair as she tried to decipher the message. A squiggly signature leapt out at her. Shane! Was it? Yes, it had to be. That was definitely an "S", though the "h" looked more like an "l". Why was his writing so peculiar? "Drugs," whispered Trish's voice in her mind. "Told you so!"

"No ... no," she mumbled out loud.

Her heart was hammering. She felt dizzy and breathless and her head started swimming as if she were about to faint. She was glad she was sitting down. As she stared at the card, the shaky letters gradually began to form into words.

Had accident. Am in Ward 10, Chadwick Hospital. Please visit. Love, Shane.

She flipped the card over. Yes, the ugly redbrick building was the hospital. She should have noticed. She turned it over again. He'd put one *X* after his name, just one, but it was a big, straggly, blotchy one like a squashed spider. She put her lips to it and kissed it, then rushed to find the phone book.

Visiting hours were from four until eight, she discovered. She made the fastest change of clothes ever, made her face up in an attempt to disguise the ravages of the last few days, scribbled a note for her mother to say she wouldn't be in for dinner, and ran all the way to the bus stop.

For once, every aspect of her journey went like clockwork. The bus came as soon as she got there, it wasn't held up in any traffic jams, the next bus was already standing at the stop as she got off the first one, and she arrived at the hospital a mere twenty minutes after leaving her house. But it had seemed like for ever.

There was a flower stall near the hospital. Viv deliberated over the spring flowers but finally chose some unusual apricot coloured carnations which reminded her of the painted desert on Shane's Valentine card.

She was shaking as she went up in the lift and approached the ward on the third floor. Spotting a nurse standing in a room by the entrance to the ward, she asked where she could find Shane Russell.

"He's over at the far end, next to last bed on the left," the nurse told her.

Viv took a deep breath and started the endless walk down the ward. Her legs felt wobbly and she seemed to be gliding along in slow motion, her eyes fixed on the motionless figure that was lying beneath the white hospital coverlet. She could see a leg in plaster attached to a pulley. A bare foot stuck out of it.

At last she reached him. He looked as if he was asleep. His eyes were closed and his face looked greyish and engraved with lines of pain. She sat on a brown plastic chair by the bed, still clutching the bunch of carnations.

His hair was uncombed, and stuck out at odd, tufty angles like a little boy's. He was wearing navy blue pyjamas. There was a large, jagged cut on his forehead. She could count the stitches in it. A yellow and black discolouration surrounded one of his eyes. His left arm was in plaster, too. She could just see the top of the cast, the rest being beneath the sheet.

She wanted to cry but no tears would come. She wanted to hug his poor, battered body, kiss his pale, dry lips, but she was fearful of waking him up in case he was in a lot of pain.

For half an hour or more she kept up her vigil at his bedside, until some noisy visitors arrived to see the person in the bed next to Shane's. Their loud, cheerful greetings woke Shane up. His eyelids flickered and a spasm of pain distorted his face before he blinked his eyes open.

Oh, the blueness of his gaze – rockpools in the summer sun, with the light glancing off them.

"Viv..." he whispered, taking his good hand out from the bedclothes and reaching out for hers. "Oh, Viv, I was so stupid."

"No, you weren't. It was me who was stupid," she said.

"I was stupid for jumping to conclusions and driving off in a foul temper and crashing the van. When Jane brought me your letter, I realized..."

"Realized what?" Viv's eyes hadn't left his for an instant. They were mesmerizing her, pulling her into their gleaming, beaming depths.

"Realized that I should have believed what I felt. Believed that you loved me as much as I loved you. I deserve these injuries—"

"No, you don't!" Viv blazed furiously. "I should have been straight with you from the start. When we started going out together, I was still seeing Jon, but it was petering out. He started seeing my friend. Who told you, anyway?"

"Nobody told me. I was on my way to see you. I couldn't wait till Thursday night, I'd already waited long enough, all those days I was at my mother's. But just as I was driving up to your house, there you were, kissing someone else. It looked like Jon."

"Yes, it was. We were saying our final goodbye, after talking everything through. We'd just agreed to stay friends."

"Well, how was I to know that? You can imagine how I felt!"

"Yes, I can, only too well," grimaced Viv. His hand was growing warmer in her grasp. "Is your foot cold?" she asked, touching the toes of the foot that stuck out from the plaster cast.

"Freezing!"

Viv bent down and unlaced the shoe that she was wearing. She took off her black sock and very carefully rolled it on to his foot.

"Ah, that's better. You've warmed it up for me. Thanks," he said. "Don't you need it to go home in?"

"I'll be reckless and take the other one off, too," she said.

"Reckless and sockless. I like that." He laughed,

then groaned and his face twisted with pain. "I must remember not to laugh," he said ruefully.

"How ... how badly hurt are you?" Viv asked anxiously.

"Oh, complicated fracture in my leg, simple one in my arm, three cracked ribs, this cut... Can you still love me with a big scar and a pair of crutches?"

"It'll fade. I'd still love you with ten big scars," Viv assured him cheefully.

"Oh, thanks! I hope that doesn't mean I've got nine more car accidents to come," he joked.

"Shush. Don't even *think* about it," Viv said.

"Do you think you could do something about these pillows for me?" he asked her. "They've got all twisted up behind my back."

He leaned forward as much as he was able while Viv did what she could to straighten them. But she had to tug and pull at them quite a lot.

"I didn't hurt you, did I?" she asked Shane anxiously.

"I think we both hurt each other," he answered quietly.

They gazed at each other for a while, both too full of complex feelings to want to speak.

Finally, it was Shane who broke the silence. "I don't think I'll be playing the guitar for a while. I don't think I'll be able to drive, either. I might be able to manage the computer with one hand. It won't stop me writing songs, though," he said.

"Not like the last one, I hope," Viv said.

"No. I've been lying here trying to think of words that rhyme with Viv. Like 'live' ... and 'forgive'."

"I think we can do both of those," Viv said.

"And love?"

"That doesn't rhyme with 'Viv'."

"It doesn't have to. Neither does 'kiss'."

His eyes were tugging at her heart. She left her chair and very gently sat down on the edge of his bed, trying not to disturb his leg. She put a hand on his shoulder and rested her cheek against his, inhaling the scent of his skin, aware of how very thin his cotton pyjamas were, so thin that she could feel the heat of his body through them, burning her hand.

"Viv..." he murmured against her lips.

"Shane..." she whispered back against his.

Then their lips stopped forming words and met, and clung. And time stopped, and nurses and patients and visitors couldn't be heard, only the pounding of their hearts and the singing of their blood and the heat and beat of love itself, enclosing them in its golden radiance. Like candle flame ... like honey ... like the brightest dawn on the warmest summer's day.

Point Romance

Caroline B. Cooney

The lives, loves and hopes of five young girls appear in this dazzling mini series:

Anne – coming to terms with a terrible secret that has changed her whole life.

Kip – everyone's best friend, but no one's dream date . . . why can't she find the right guy?

Molly – out for revenge against the four girls she has always been jealous of . . .

Emily – whose secure and happy life is about to be threatened by disaster.

Beth Rose – dreaming of love but wondering if it will ever become a reality.

Follow the five through their last years of high school, in four brilliant titles: *Saturday Night, Last Dance, New Year's Eve,* and *Summer Nights*

Point Romance

Look out for this heartwarming Point Romance mini series:

First Comes Love

by Jennifer Baker

Can their happiness last?

When eighteen-year-old college junior Julie
Miller elopes with Matt Collins, a wayward and
rebellious biker, no one has high hopes for a
happy ending. They're penniless, cut off from
their parents, homeless and too young. But no
one counts on the strength of their love for one
another and commitment of their vows.

Four novels, *To Have and To Hold*, *For Better
For Worse*, *In Sickness and in Health*, and *Till
Death Do Us Part*, follow Matt and Julie through
their first year of marriage.

Once the honeymoon is over, they have to deal
with the realities of life. Money worries,
tensions, jealousies, illness, accidents, and the
most heartbreaking decision of their lives.
Can their love survive?

Four novels to touch your heart . . .

A terrifying series from Point Horror!

NIGHTMARE HALL

Where college is a

scream . . .

High on a hill overlooking Salem
University, hidden in shadows and
shrouded in mystery, sits Nightingale Hall.

Nightmare Hall, the students call it.

Because that's where the terror began . . .

Don't miss the spine-tingling thrillers in
the Nightmare Hall series –

The Silent Scream
The Roommate
Deadly Attraction
The Wish
Guilty

P●INT CRiME

If you like Point Horror, you'll love Point Crime!

A murder has been committed . . . Whodunnit?
Was it the teacher, the schoolgirl, or the best friend? An
exciting series of crime novels, with tortuous plots and lots
of suspects, designed to keep the reader guessing till the
very last page.

Kiss of Death
School for Death
Peter Beere

Avenging Angel
Break Point
Final Cut
Shoot the Teacher
The Beat:
Missing Person
David Belbin

Baa Baa Dead Sheep
Jill Bennett

A Dramatic Death
Margaret Bingley

Driven to Death
Anne Cassidy

Overkill
Alane Ferguson

Death Penalty
Dennis Hamley

Concrete Evidence
The Smoking Gun
Malcolm Rose

Look out for:

Patsy Kelly Investigates:
A Family Affair
Anne Cassidy

The Beat:
Black and Blue
David Belbin

Deadly Music
Dennis Hamley

Point

Pointing the way forward

More compelling reading from top authors.

Point Horror Fans Beware!

*Available now from Point Horror are tales
for the midnight hour . . .*

THE *Point Horror* TAPES

Two Point Horror stories are terrifyingly
brought to life in a chilling dramatisation
featuring actors from The Story Circle and
with spine tingling sound effects.

Point Horror as you've never heard
it before . . .

**HALLOWEEN NIGHT
TRICK OR TREAT
THE CEMETERY
DREAM DATE**

available now on audiotape at your
nearest bookshop.

Listen if you dare . . .